Waiting
Under
Water

Riel Nason

Waiting Under Water

Scholastic Canada Ltd.

Toronto New York London Auckland Sydney
Mexico City New Delhi Hong Kong Buenos Aires

Scholastic Canada Ltd.
604 King Street West, Toronto, Ontario M5V 1E1, Canada

Scholastic Inc.
557 Broadway, New York, NY 10012, USA

Scholastic Australia Pty Limited
PO Box 579, Gosford, NSW 2250, Australia

Scholastic New Zealand Limited
Private Bag 94407, Botany, Manukau 2163, New Zealand

Scholastic Children's Books
Euston House, 24 Eversholt Street, London NW1 1DB, UK

www.scholastic.ca

Library and Archives Canada Cataloguing in Publication

Title: Waiting under water / Riel Nason.

Names: Nason, Riel, 1969- author.

Identifiers: Canadiana (print) 20190235365 | Canadiana (ebook) 20190235381 |
ISBN 9781443175135 (softcover) | ISBN 9781443175142 (ebook)

Classification: LCC PS8627.A7775 W34 2020 | DDC jC813/.6—dc23

Cover photo and throughout ©: Delstudio/Dreamstime;
All other photos © Shutterstock.com.

6 5 4 3 2 1   Printed in Canada 114   20 21 22 23 24

For Mom and Dad

Chapter 1

I'm making sea glass.

It's here on our beach, way back behind my house, waiting under the water like a rainbow broken into bits. What I mean is, when the tide goes out, it will be almost the same as when the rain stops — then you'll see the colours left on the shore, bright and shining in the sun.

My glass is red and dark blue, green, amethyst and amber, white and turquoise. It's parts of vases and plates and bowls that I bought at yard sales and smashed with a hammer (yes, it was fun). My best friend, Willa, gave me what was left of her piggy bank after she broke it to get the money out. Plus, I have the pieces of what used to be my grandmother's favourite pink candy dish. Thanks to her twenty-pound orange cat, Mr. McPuff. One day he swung his huge fluffy tail like a baseball bat and hit a home run with the dish, right off her kitchen table.

I keep my glass in a giant sack made of ten window screens all attached and sewn end to end. Dad helped me put it together. There are small rocks and sand in with it, and the whole contraption lies flat, anchored in place right below the tide line.

Really, I'm not making the sea glass, the ocean is. The waves do the work. Mother Nature is the big boss and I'm just the project manager, checking in on things now and then. The Bay of Fundy has the highest tides in the whole world, and they keep moving the glass around, pushing and pulling it, tumbling and swirling it, over and over. The screens let the water and sand go in and out but keep my rainbow from getting lost. The sharp edges of the glass rub against sand and rocks and get smoother, the teeniest bit at a time. Pointy, jagged parts become rounded. Dangerous shards turn into polished gems.

Of course it takes a while. The regular sea glass people find around here and on beaches all over the world is usually at least ten or twenty years old, maybe more. But when I first started the project four years ago, when I was eight, I didn't know how long I'd have to wait. I thought maybe the sea glass would be ready for the Science Fair in grade five. Then maybe grade six. Except it wasn't and that was fine. It's not something that can be sped up or rushed; the time it takes is the time it takes.

Dad says my patience is very mature and that I'm an "old soul." I didn't know what it meant when I was younger. So he explained that it was as if the soul or spirit inside me already had some worldly experience, and that I could be pretty relaxed about everything this time through because I'd lived a life before. I thought it sounded so awesome and special, like part of me was recycled — and recycling and reusing is so crazy important for the earth. Dad says I can calmly go with the flow — like the flow of the water, in and out. Think about it: the tide never forgets what it's doing. It doesn't worry about how long it's taking, or try to speed up.

But time mostly goes slow for kids anyway. I never believed the old ladies who would smile at me in the grocery store and then say to Mom (like it was some legally required statement I heard it so much), "Oh, enjoy it while you can, they grow up so fast." Years passing by wasn't a big deal. I didn't consider it.

Or at least not until two months ago. That's when Dad called Mom and my brother, Jacob, and me into the dining room for a family meeting and made the big announcement that would lead to The Point of No Return. Now I track time. All the time, all of the time. Sometimes I count up, adding days together, but more often I subtract. I count down, think of what's been used. Ten, nine, eight. Deep breath. I like to know what's gone and how much I have left. I'm not sure if it helps me feel any better about the whole situation or not.

But here on our beach is the best place to forget everything for a while and only think of how beautiful it is. I've come down to the shore my whole life. In our living room there's a framed picture of my tiny baby footprints in this sand. Along the beach there are patches of grey and almost-purplish rocks shaped like perfect ovals. Some are speckled with white dots, so they look like petrified eggs laid by a prehistoric bird. As I walk the waves come in, swell and crash, then ripple and froth to my feet. I love listening to the water.

I'm taking the really, really long way back home, walking a giant loop. I go from our beach down to the public beach. It's busy this afternoon, like always. You can tell who the tourists are. They have a lot of stuff with them — towels and blankets and umbrellas and shade tents and folding chairs.

They usually have big red or blue coolers of food and drinks. At the shore they freak out as if the water is made of just-melted ice cubes. Then when they leave they take a few of the egg-shaped rocks with them. The rocks make big bulges in the bottom of their beach bags.

I also see two men I don't recognize as any of the 474 people who live in our village of St. David's, and who really don't look like tourists either. First of all, they're both wearing jeans, which are definitely not beach clothes. Pants are pretty tricky to swim in. Their shirts are matching green golf shirts with white trim on the collars and sleeves. One of them is writing things down on a clipboard. The other has two different fancy cameras hanging across his chest. That guy is pointing, marking out the edges of a certain area of the beach like he's trying to imagine something there. They talk and nod to each other as I get closer.

"Or down by those caves might work. As long as it's big enough and not too shadowy to shoot," one says as I'm walking by.

The other man nods. "It would be fine for just the two of them, and I bet Anne would love it. You know Phil doesn't care as long as she's happy. But once the guests arrive . . ." He stops talking and seems to think for a bit. "Well, maybe, if we figure there's enough room for everyone. We'll go see. We definitely want to make it a day to remember."

They must be planning for a wedding. There have been lots here. It's more proof of how special and perfect this stretch of beach is. I hope the bride chooses near the sea caves. I would. You know, hypothetically. (I haven't even decided if I'll ever get married, let alone any time soon.) They aren't scary deep caves, just scooped out areas of the reddish cliffs. It's like a giant scraped away bits here and there with his fingernails, then pushed his thumb in hard a couple of places. Actually, the waves made the caves by *eroding* bits of the rock and you can only see them all at low tide. But everyone from around here knows enough to take the tide into consideration when they're planning any event near the water. Anne might be the vice-principal's daughter, who I know is getting married this summer.

I go across the public parking lot. At the edge there's a little ice cream stand that looks like a lighthouse. It's called Frosty Point Light Cool Cones and Treatery (long name, I know). The building is white with freshly painted red trim.

I start to walk down the main street. Most of the

houses in St. David's are more than a hundred years old. Lots of them are big too, with gables and turrets and plenty of gingerbread-house icing decoration along the roof. A couple have little porches up high, outside an attic window. Those are called "widow's walks" and were made so wives could see way out onto the ocean and watch for their husbands' ships to return home from their dangerous journeys.

I go by a white church with a tall steeple and then past another smaller one that isn't a church at all anymore but has been changed into a coffee shop and craft gallery.

Along the sidewalk are giant flowerpots in front of every other telephone pole. They have big bunches of red and white geraniums and pretty periwinkle-blue flowers that hang down. When I go by the tiny brick building that's both the post office and village hall, there are more flowers in a bed out front. Dark orange marigolds planted in the shape of a lobster seem to have popped up overnight.

The school has a brand new bright yellow New Brunswick flag (the other one was really faded), even though students are out for the summer. And "Fran's Fish and Hips," which is what everyone calls it because the "C" falls off at least once a summer and Fran and friends never seem to be in any hurry to replace it, is "Fran's Fish and Chips" again. Good as new.

All the little improvements are St. David's way of looking its best for the visitors who come in July and August, like the tourists I just saw at the beach. We're not a big, rockin', must-see destination where people come and stay for days at a time. There are plenty of other seaside places like that — with double-page spreads in the New Brunswick guidebook advertising their fancy food festivals, big outdoor concerts or nationally known sandcastle-building contests.

People stop here for an afternoon, maybe a picnic, a quick swim, an ice cream, a browse in our two craft shops and galleries, a quick stroll down this street. Not much exciting happens here, which is fine with me. (Although I certainly wouldn't object if something did.) St. David's is keeping calm, cool and collected. And having my own personal backyard beach to hang out on any time I want is awesome.

When I'm almost home, I notice one more late-breaking village improvement. Except maybe I shouldn't call it that since I know for sure it's not on the usual St. David's summer to-do list. In fact, I've never seen it done before and Jacob always joked it would be a sign of the Apocalypse if it ever took place. Across the street a man is taking down old Mrs. Wright's Christmas lights. Yes, it is summer and, yes, I said Christmas lights. They've been up permanently for years and years and years — probably since before I was born. They used to circle every window and the front door, then go along the porch and roof. Now the cords are all criss-crossed, saggy and dangling so the white house looks like a big dot-to-dot drawing a kindergartener did a messy job on.

As I walk through my front yard I can tell that the man up the ladder is Bobby McIsaac, who works for the village. (He's basically the one-man St. David's Parks and Recreation department.) I don't get it. I wonder what the deal is?

Then, since I'm not paying attention to where I am going, I bang right into something on my lawn. It's a "For Sale" sign. I hurt my shoulder bumping into the post and then the hanging sign swings forward and back and spanks me on the butt. Owww. Great. I look around but I don't think Bobby or anyone else saw it happen. The sign is another new thing, a change, but it is unequivocally not — in no way ever — an improvement.

And I know all about the what and when and why

of it even though I wish I didn't. It also has nothing to do with anyone except our family.

I feel a twitch in my throat and I make a loud "Hummph" sound that I can't control. "Hummph. Hummph." It's not a hiccup though. I take a long deep breath in through my nose and blow it out slowly through my mouth. Again. And again.

"Hummph."

Jacob was right. For Sale Sign of the Apocalypse indeed.

Chapter 2

So we're moving. And not like down the street, but moving away. All the way to Toronto away. The Point of No Return is the day we absolutely have to be there so I can start school. Really, we'll move before then; I doubt that on the first day of class I'll be rushing off a plane and jumping into a taxi, screaming, "Toronto Middle School and step on it!" like a scene from a movie.

Our Likely Departure Date is at least a week and a half before The Point of No Return. Also known as Impending Doom Coming Way Too Soon. But I'm hoping every single remaining day of the summer is here rather than there. The house better not suddenly sell tomorrow. I plan on staying as long as I can.

We do have to go though. For sure. It's an unexpected twist in my life that's so twisted it's more like a big, tangled knot. Dad works for a company that closed its Atlantic branch. Everyone who worked there had their job taken away completely, except Dad, who was offered a big promotion and lots more money to go work at the company's head office in Toronto. He thought about it a long, long, loooonnnng time before he said yes. He and Mom stayed up late at night whispering about it for weeks. He even looked for a different job here first. But no luck.

Moving wasn't anybody's first choice, but now that the decision is made, my parents never question it and they try to sell it to me as the new and improved Best. Idea. Ever! Like it's *Robinson Family: Version 2.0.* Please update and install immediately. I know it's not fair to be mad at Dad for being great at his job, but I totally am. Maybe I can "get excited about this new adventure" like Mom says. Maybe I can also remember, as Mom suggests, that I'm certainly not the only one in the family giving things up. (Mom is giving up her job here as an educational assistant at the school.)

Maybe I can come to accept the move, using my proper perspective on things as the wise old soul I am. Or maybe not. I can still secretly hope for a sudden million-dollar inheritance from a long-lost relative or a brand new business to open here and hire Dad. Yeah. Or I could hope to wake up tomorrow with the ability to fly. I think my life would have been better if Dad had been laid off like everyone else.

I go inside. Mom's in the kitchen with the real estate agent, Karly Cook. Her slogan is "Listed by Karly Cook? Yes, it's worth a look!" And Karly herself is pretty hard not to take at least a significant glance at. She seems six inches taller than she really is thanks to high heels on her feet and high hair on her head. She wears sequins during daylight hours. Her entire wardrobe ranges in colour from pink to fuchsia. I think she must order all her clothing online, maybe from a store in Las Vegas. I highly doubt she's an old soul, but if she was here on earth in another life, I bet it was as a flamingo.

"Hope," Mom says. "I'm glad you're back. Karly and I still have to finish a few things, but then we'll make supper."

Karly turns and smiles at me. Her teeth are so white it's like there are little spotlights along her gums beaming up at them. I almost wonder if they glow in the dark, like if she gets up in the night for a snack she just grins to guide her way to the kitchen. Karly's holding papers. There are more that Mom's signing on the table in front of them.

"Go take a peek in your dad's office, on his desk,"

Mom says. "There's something there for you. We'll only be ten minutes tops."

"Okay," I say. I smile back at Karly.

Dad's office is at the front of the house with a nice view of the street. He used to work from home two days a week, doing everything by computer, and then the other three days he drove into Saint John. The room is big with a huge antique oak desk. Dad also had tall bookcases with glass doors crammed full of books, but they aren't here now. Karly wanted us to "stage" our house for selling. That meant decluttering it enough that it looks half-empty and boring. It's so anyone interested in buying it can more easily imagine what it might look like filled with their own furniture and things.

I think we should have left it as is, so it is easier to imagine it as an actual home rather than as a doctor's waiting room. Not too many people love going to the doctor, so I can't see the place giving anyone a good vibe about it now. I'd lean more toward feeling nervous and germy. But that's me. Karly claims the current state of our house will make it sell faster and for a better price.

Lots of our furniture is already in the garage. Plenty of our personal things are packed up too. Pictures are off the walls. The colourful blankets

Mom crocheted are gone from our couches.

Plus Dad is missing. Although I can't blame Karly for that.

He's already up in Toronto, working. He's also trying to find us the perfect place to move into. He's been there three weeks and tries to make it sound super exciting every time he calls. He says there are so many things to do and see we can be like tourists for years! Every weekend can be a new adventure!

I look on the desk like Mom told me to. As I figured, there's a printed confirmation for my flight to visit Dad next week. Just looking at the ticket I swear I can feel time speeding up. I can hear it whizzing by my ear and sense it rippling the air all around me.

"Hummph. Hummph." Deep breath.

It'll be my first time on a plane. And it will be great to see Dad. It will be fun to do everything he has planned — except of course the house-hunting part. I've never been to Toronto and it really does sound like a great place to *visit*. But all those times Dad said we could be like tourists for years, well, it doesn't work like that. Not even close. Being away, going, seeing, doing, having adventures is great, but part of every trip and what makes you a tourist by definition is that you eventually get to come back home and sleep in your own bed again. Dad seems to have forgotten that. There's a word for what happens to tourists when they stay away too long: *homesickness*. Home. Sickness. And there's only one way it can be cured.

I sit in Dad's big leather chair. I spin around once, twice, then stop before I get dizzy. I lean way back, which gives me a perfect view out the front window. Mrs. Wright's house looks completely different. I wonder if people will still call her Mrs. Claus behind her back without the Christmas lights up. It's strange, but it's like she and Santa suddenly broke up, then she threw away all his stuff. I don't get it. There must be some special reason it happened now. She didn't die; I saw her this morning. And why was Bobby doing it? I wonder if the village is trying to look extra good this summer for some reason.

Karly laughs in the kitchen. It's the giggle of a cartoon princess. The sound makes everything click into place in my brain. Of course. Mystery solved. Taking down the Christmas lights is more of Karly's "staging." It's to make the view out our front window look good to any potential buyers. Karly probably smiled at Bobby, bright and wide and twinkly, and then promised Mrs. Wright that of course he'd put all the lights back when the snow flies.

Just because my life is changing so dramatically doesn't mean I need to think every other little change around here has a bigger meaning. Note to self: Chill. Relax and do your best to enjoy your last summer in St. David's. I take a few deep breaths, blow them out slowly. Okay. Better.

But I still wish I could go smile at Bobby and make him put all the lights back. I'm not a fan of anything that might make our house sell faster.

Chapter 3

After supper I walk down to Willa's house. Her house is The Sea Captain's Inn. It's mansion-sized. Half of it has ten guest rooms, and her family lives in the other half. Willa and I have been friends almost our whole lives. We met when we were two and connected because we had a lot in common. You know, like we both loved playing with blocks and jumping in puddles and going on the baby swings in the playground. Pretty standard little kid stuff. But I was lucky that Willa and I got paired up. Her mom, Lee, and my mom used to take us to storytime at the library. That was where all four of us came together and Mom and Lee became friends too. Now Willa and I have our whole history in common, years of fun memories. When I move, I will miss her most of all.

Mom tries to make me feel better about the whole situation by reminding me how much modern technology helps people stay in touch. She says Willa and I can still see each other and chat every day — on a computer screen. We can be in almost constant contact if we want. Mom says if she had moved when she was a kid, it would have been like she fell off the edge of the earth. Computers were a new thing back then, barely anyone had one at home and nobody had thought of the internet yet. Phones were attached to walls! Mom says maybe — maybe — a quick long-distance phone call to a friend might have been rarely allowed, but they were very expensive (even on Sunday, which was the one day there was a discount). Letter writing would have been the solution. There would have been a wait of days, if not weeks, between mail. Seriously. So the main message I took away from the conversation is that it could be worse. Except it already seems bad enough.

As I walk up the lane, Willa is sitting on the front steps and Lee is weeding the mulch bed around the purple lilac bushes. Lee turns and says hello, but then before she can say anything else, Willa jumps down the steps and puts her arm around me. It's all in one quick, graceful movement. Willa is a highland dancer. She's really good and wins medals and trophies at competitions all the time. You know that quote, "Dance like no one is watching"? Well, Willa dances like everyone is watching. She's competitive, but in a positive way. Plus, she looks like a beautiful Scottish souvenir doll when she wears her blue tartan kilt and velvet jacket and her long blond hair is braided and twisted into a bun.

Willa gets us each a glass of lemonade and then we go up to the widow's walk outside the attic. It's our special place to be alone and we've come up here for years. It's just big enough to fit the folding lawn chairs we've placed side by side. There's a railing too, so it's not scary even though we're very high up. The view is incredible. You can see the whole village, way down to the public beach and so far out into the ocean that the water and sky blend into each other.

"Ah, much better," Willa says, and plops into her chair. She takes a long drink of her lemonade. "I'll be so glad when our housekeeper gets back next week. Helping Mom tidy the guest rooms and then practising dance too is exhausting in this heat." She puts her hand on her forehead and leans back as if she's swooning. I laugh. She's exaggerating big time. She has more energy than anyone I know. Lee jokes that when Willa's old enough to drink coffee, she'll be unstoppable.

"Hey!" she says. "Seriously." She manages to keep a straight face for all of three seconds, then laughs too. "So while I was here working away, I suppose you were lying on the beach."

"Maybe," I say. "For a while."

Willa rolls her eyes. "Figures."

"I did go in swimming too."

"Ha, ha," Willa says. "What else is new."

I shrug, then take a drink of my lemonade.

A few seconds pass. The joking's done.

"The 'For Sale' sign went on the house today," I say.

"Really?" Willa scrunches her nose. She looks a little down. But the gloom lasts only a second, then she smiles.

"We've still got lots of summer for fun first," she says. "Hanging on the beach. Going for ice cream. Sleepovers. Plenty of time." She smiles more. And I know she is doing it for me, being positive and happy, not wanting to wreck the time we have left together being sad. But oh I wish she'd say how much she'll miss me. Just so I can be a hundred percent sure she will. I mean, we don't have to sob for days or trade pieces of each other's hair or anything, but she also doesn't have to be quite so strong.

I'm going to miss her so much it feels like a giant

bookcase tips over and crushes my chest whenever I think about it. Willa seems to be totally taking it all "in stride," as my dad would say. I really think a couple of tears would be okay.

A "hummph" sound slips out. Then another. Willa doesn't say anything about it. She knows.

I take a drink of lemonade.

"Hey, why don't you sleep over tonight?" Willa asks. "I'll even turn your bed down nice, fluff your pillow and everything since I'm the current house-keeper."

"Wow, an offer I can't refuse," I say.

"At your service." She stands up and curtseys in front of me.

Willa truly is special. Like one of a kind. Something else that makes me feel as if a giant bookcase is squishing me is when I think about how on earth I'm going to find another friend even half as good as her. Sometimes I wonder what awful thing my old soul might have done in another life that I'm being punished like this now.

Chapter 4

Days since summer vacation started: 27
Days until Likely Departure Date: 34
Days until The Point of No Return: 46

I have breakfast in the glassed-in porch at the front of The Inn along with the other guests. It's serve-yourself, but Willa is helping Lee replenish the food, clear tables and wipe up spills. It's a sunny day and the room is filled with light. I'm sitting in a corner at a table by myself eating a super yummy waffle with real maple syrup (The Inn is fancy like that) and watching the TV attached to the wall. The sound is muted, but that's okay because it would be hard to hear with the other guests chatting anyway.

It's a show called *Rise and Shine Canada*. I've watched parts of it before. The hosts are a man and a woman and they interview guests, with breaks every half-hour for news and weather. The woman is talking to a guest about sunscreen. They are rubbing white blobs of it on the back of their hands. From their facial expressions they seem way more excited about it than they should be. When that part is over, a "Happy Fiftieth Birthday, George" banner pops up at the bottom of the screen and the woman beckons someone off to the side to come over. A man in a green shirt walks onscreen. Another man follows him with a cake.

"Excuse me." An older couple has come up to my table and the man is talking to me. "Is it all right if we join you here?"

All the other seats in the room are basically full. There are three empty chairs at my table.

I nod. "Sure."

They sit down. They seem very nice and chatty. They're visiting from Cornwall, Ontario. When they ask where I'm from and I say actually right here and that I'm friends with The Inn's owners, they have lots of nice things to say about their stay. After a while there's a lull in the conversation and I go back to eating my waffle. The woman looks up to watch the TV, but then starts talking again.

"You know, Anne is really lovely in person," she says. "I met her last year."

I don't know who or what she's talking about so I just nod.

"That was at the literacy fundraiser you went to, wasn't it?" the man says. "Too bad they couldn't have had both Anne and Phil there."

Anne and Phil? I think I know them for some reason. Why are their names familiar? I've clued in that the older couple is talking about the hosts of the TV show, but that's not what I'm remembering. I look back at the screen. The show is going to a commercial break and the camera cuts to George the birthday boy eating a piece of cake. He drops some white icing on his green shirt.

That's it.

Anne and Phil were the names I heard the men on the beach mention, the men who I thought were planning the set-up for a wedding. They were wearing the exact same shirts as George. I remember the white trim around the sleeves. And I bet anything that if I had looked more closely, the embroidered logo would have said *Rise and Shine Canada*.

But, what? Why?

Wait, wait. No. What had they said on the beach? Well, maybe. But here?

"Do you watch the show a lot?" I ask the couple. "Do they ever leave the studio and film somewhere else?"

"Well now, I don't know about that, not that I can think of," the man says.

"No, no." The woman disagrees with him. "Don't you remember when they did that Winter Wonderland week and they went to different cities that had winter carnivals?"

"Oh, now you're right. They did, didn't they? My old memory isn't quite what—" the man starts, but I say great, thanks, push back my chair, scan the room for Willa or Lee, and jump up before he finishes.

Lee walks back into the porch with a fresh pitcher of juice.

"Hey, Hope, Willa's just in the kitchen loading the dishwasher, then you two can get on with your summer adventures."

"Thanks, but I wanted to ask you something first." I decide to flat-out go for it. "Is *Rise and Shine Canada* going to be filming something here?"

"*Rise and Shine Canada*?" She says it like she hasn't heard of the show before. But they play it in the porch every morning. Nice try, Lee. She knows something, I'm sure.

"Yes, *Rise and Shine Canada*, are they coming here?"

This time Lee looks around and then shushes

me. She points to the hotel foyer. I follow her out there.

"First," she whispers, "why are you asking? How do you know?"

"I saw men from the show down at the beach. They were planning something — something big."

Lee nods. "Fair enough then," she whispers. "There will be a village meeting tonight. Emails are going out this morning telling people to be there but not why, so until then, top secret. Total, total secret, like zip." She pretends to zipper her lips closed. "Although I know of course you'll burst if you don't tell Willa." Lee looks around to check that no one is close enough to overhear her. "They're going to be broadcasting live."

"Really? Why? Why here? And when?"

"Shhhhh," Lee says. "No more details for now. Only a few of us business owners and people at the village office know. But tonight . . ." Then she lifts her hands and wiggles her fingers. She tries to make her voice sound magical: ". . . all will be revealed."

I can't believe it. A live TV show filming. One that's shown all across Canada! There's never been anything like that done anywhere near here before. And I might even be on TV. Please, please be soon, while I still live here. I can't stand the thought of missing one more thing. It would so great to have something genuinely exciting to look forward to, rather than every future event in my life being tinged with dread.

Please, universe, work with me here. If you can't change my relocation situation at least give me this one little thing. Please, please, pretty please.

Chapter 5

I get Willa to follow me to the farthest corner of The Inn's backyard. It's a good idea because she lets out a little squeal when she hears the news. She asks me about a hundred questions that I can't answer.

Then we agree to stay quiet and simmered down about the whole thing. We'll see each other at the meeting. Willa will be housekeeping and practising dance again. I'm going to see my neighbour Em, who lives across the street from us (next to Mrs. Wright).

Em's in the big front window of her place when I walk up the driveway. She's twenty-seven and the most beautiful woman in probably the whole history of the village. She's tall and she has long, wavy dark red hair and blue eyes. But her beauty isn't the best thing about her — not even close.

Em is a textile artist. Her house is her studio and gallery too. She has a giant long-arm quilting machine that she finishes her quilts on. She said it cost more than a lot of people's cars.

I can see her standing, holding the big controller with one hand on each grip. It looks like something that would steer a spaceship in *Star Wars*. Really, it only moves the tiny sewing needle across the quilt on the frame below it. Em's let me try it a few times and it's fun to use. It's like the needle is a pencil and the stitched thread is the line you draw.

I go in her gallery door. It's rigged to ring a bell by her machine when it opens. The gallery is filled with brightly coloured quilts hanging on the walls. Em uses small fabric pieces and sews them together randomly, making the whole quilt up as she goes along, not repeating the same pattern anywhere. Not everyone understands her quilts and once she heard an old lady say it looked like she dumped a garbage bag of fabric scraps on the floor and sewed them together just the way they landed. So Em smiled and told her maybe she'd try that sometime. (Ha, ha. Em is quick like that.)

I love that Em talks to me about art and how it is important to be different and "wildly creative" and make exactly what you want. She knows all about the history of traditional quilting, because she says it is important to never forget where you came from. But as long as she understands and respects that, she's fine if a few people think her quilts are strange. Most people are totally wowed by them. She's a real artist and people from all over the world have bought her quilts.

"Aha! My apprentice has arrived," Em says as she walks toward me. Her tabby cat, Stitches, follows behind her, then runs ahead and rubs against my legs.

"Do you have any packages for me to get ready?" I ask.

"Only a few, some orders from the website for notecards. Then did you want to work on your quilt?"

"For sure," I say.

Em leads me back to her studio space. I stop at the big desk with her computer. Stitches jumps up and gets into a little basket he has there.

"Let me know when you're done," she says. She goes back to her big long-arm machine.

I'm not actually Em's apprentice, but I do help her do some packaging and mailing. I'm kind of her part-time shipping department. I like to have a way to help her since she taught me to sew and she lets me use her fabric to make whatever I want.

I get the orders finished fast, but someone comes into the gallery before I can tell Em. So I head over to where I'm working on my quilt, which will be a surprise gift for Willa before I move. The pieces I've cut so far are on what's called a "design wall." It's a big square of white flannel that I can smooth the fabric on and reposition everything as much as I want before sewing it all together. The quilt is my own design, an original one-of-a-kind. I decided to make it look like the ocean for the big top section and then at the bottom will be the shoreline with a few rocks and pieces of sea glass.

I almost have the ocean part done. I cut long strips of a whole bunch of different blue fabrics. Em suggested I cut a few of them a bit crooked to add more variety. It was a genius idea because now the strips look like abstract waves.

"It's coming along great," Em says when she comes up behind me. "You've made nice fabric choices and it's got wonderful composition and movement."

I feel myself blush. Em treats me like a real artist too.

"Willa will dream of the ocean when she's wrapped up in this. And remember what I told you about the first person to sleep under a new quilt?"

"They get to make a wish," I say.

"They do. Not everyone knows that, but it's

another special sewn-in feature of a handmade quilt. You are giving her this work of art made by you, using your creativity and time and effort, like a piece of yourself really, to stay in St. David's. And you're giving her a wish too."

I have to look down for a minute.

A piece of myself to stay in St. David's. Oh, Em, I know you didn't mean to remind me, but why only a piece?

"Hummph. Hummph."

I know what I'd wish for if I got a quilt.

Chapter 6

Mom's in the kitchen on the phone when I get back from Em's. She's talking to Jacob. I yell hello to him. He graduated from high school in June and he's away planting trees up north as his summer job.

The timing of our family move worked out way, waaaaay better for him. He's going to university in the fall and will live in residence there. His friends from St. David's are mostly going to be away next year too. So it doesn't matter to him if our family lives here or Toronto. All it means is that he will fly home at Christmas rather than drive. I also heard his friends saying how cool it would be to have a place to stay in the city. They'd totally go up for a weekend.

What would have helped was if Jacob was a year younger. Then if Mom and Dad had told him he'd have to start a new school in a new city — especially with only one year left — he would have felt like a whole library of books fell on his chest. It would have been two against two in the family. I'm not sure if it would have ultimately changed Mom and Dad's mind, but it might have.

As annoying as Jacob can sometimes be, I already miss him. He's number one on what I know will soon be my very long Missing Persons List. Other summers we'd go swimming together or walk down to Frosty Point Light to get ice cream. He's really good at thinking up silly, fun things to do — like last summer when he made Willa and me a long obstacle course down on the beach. And although I wouldn't tell him, he's got a great sense of humour. We still message back and forth a lot, but it's not the same. Jacob being gone has been enough of an adjustment family-wise without adding in this whole big move. Not only will I not have any friends in Toronto, I won't even have him.

I decide to make a smoothie as a snack, but after I search "hard and wise" (which is a family joke because when I was younger that's what I thought the expression was instead of "far and wide") for the blender, it isn't anywhere. (Something else that's missing. Figures.) I think it was a casualty of Karly's staging and I bet it's in a box in the garage now. I have a banana in solid form instead. Mom finishes her phone call and sits across the table from me.

"I wanted to talk to you about the house being for sale now. I know the sign was a surprise yesterday," she starts.

Ah yes, the sign. I remember how I kicked it on the way into the house.

"I realized there was something you might not understand a hundred percent and I wanted to explain. I want you to know that even though it's listed, you don't have to worry that all of a sudden it's going to sell and we have to move earlier than we planned. When you sell a house, the buyer and the seller agree on something called a closing date, which is when the deal goes through and you officially move. I told Karly we didn't want a closing date until at least the middle of August. That's the soonest we'd agree to go. Okay?"

Relief. I get up and hug Mom. "Okay." I quickly do the math in my head. "Good." I mean not *good*, but good considering everything. That falls right around our Likely Departure Date anyway.

She kisses my cheek. She smiles, but looks a teeny bit sad underneath. "Lots of time for summer fun with no worries. Enjoy your days. Promise?" She sounds like Willa.

"I'll try. I will."

"And you know something special is happening soon, right? You know about the meeting tonight, and what's being announced?"

"Yeah, I do," I say. "But wait, how do you know I know?"

"Lee told me you figured it out when she called this morning," Mom says. So obviously the top-secret zip-it rule didn't apply to Lee.

"Actually, that's the reason the sign went on the house early. Karly's idea. In case the show's soon. Probably lots of people will be coming in to watch the filming and that's lots of extra people to notice it's for sale."

"Hummph. Hummph. Okay," I say. "Hummph."

"But we'll be here for the summer, same as always, lots of fun," she says.

"Okay," I repeat.

Mom looks at me as if she's about to say something else. I think I even see her lips start to form a word, but then she changes her mind.

She smiles and nods. Nods and nods — like she's not only convincing me everything is going great, but herself too.

Chapter 7

The meeting is in the school gym. Mom and I arrive fifteen minutes early but it's already crammed with people. It's roasting hot. Like giant-Christmas-dinner-turkey roasting hot. The side door is propped open with the cart that holds the volleyballs but it's not helping. There are chairs set up, and all but the last two rows are mostly full. Basically, ninety percent of the whole village is here. Or it sure seems so anyway.

Somehow Lee and Willa managed to get seats right near the front and saved two for us. Mom sits beside Lee and I sit beside Willa. An older couple is on the other side of me. Behind us are two of my least favourite girls from school. Their names are Brooklyn and Madison and they are lifelong best friends like Willa and I, but are a meaner, bossier version. I ignore them.

Mayor Rose is standing at the front, near the

stage. She's a retired nurse and looks like a perfect storybook grandmother — curly silver hair, slightly plump and always smiling. After what seems like forever, she heads to the microphone. Willa grabs my hand and squeezes it.

"Good evening, everyone," Rose starts. "Thank you all for coming. I'm sure you're wondering what this exciting news is that brings us here tonight. All I ask is that everyone hold their questions until the end. I have a lot of information and details and I know everyone's already sweating in here, so if you just let me go straight through it, we'll be all the faster. Now, who's curious?"

A few claps and whistles.

"I said, who's curious?"

It's a way louder response this time. Willa and I clap, scream and stamp our feet. Then when everyone starts to "bring it down a few nachos" (another expression I misheard as a kid; I think my ears used to sometimes get filled with mini avalanches of wax) she goes on.

"Okay," Rose says. "I'm sure everyone is familiar with the show *Rise and Shine Canada*. It's on every weekday morning, shown all across the country. It films in Toronto — usually — except for this coming Monday when they'll be filming here!"

Monday? This is Friday! Finally something fun to look forward to!

There's a second or two of shocked silence, then whispers, then applause.

"So why? Well, next week they're doing a feature called Canada's Tiniest Treasures. They've chosen five small villages, all with populations less than five hundred, that they think people would enjoy learning more about. Since we're the location that's farthest east, they're starting here Monday. I have no idea how they chose us, but let's make them happy they did.

"They're going to have six guests total — five of them are local guests who I'll tell you about in a minute. They also sent a producer and cameraman the other day to take pictures and film some short clips to use going in and out of commercial breaks."

I turn and nod to Willa. That was who I saw on the beach. I wonder where else they went before they left.

"Hummph." Great, not now. I raise my hand to my mouth pretending it was a little cough.

"Hummph. Hummph." I can't control it. And covering my mouth doesn't really muffle the sound much.

I hear giggling behind me.

"Hummph."

More laughter. I'm sure it's Brooklyn and Madison. Willa turns to me and shakes her head. Then she swivels around and gives them a dirty look.

I take a deep, even breath in through my nose and blow it out slowly through my mouth. Again. And again.

Rose announces a lot more details. She describes how the stage will be on the beach. Everyone should be in their seats by 6:30 a.m. because filming starts at 7:00 a.m. sharp. There will definitely be some shots of the crowd on TV, so everyone should look their best.

"And on that note," Rose says. "I'm going to call up our village librarian, Miss Watson, now."

"Thank you, Rose," she says. "We definitely want our village pride to show. Tomorrow starting at 10:00 a.m. in the library we'll be making signs for anyone who'd like one. I have ample supplies; I just need helpers. I'm hoping to see many of our young people come out. Could I have a show of hands if you think you'll be able to help?"

Willa and I look at each other, then raise our arms in perfect synchronization. I love making posters.

Miss Watson smiles and scans the crowd. "Wonderful!" she says. "I'll see you all tomorrow."

"I can't wait," I whisper to Willa. Then because I've stopped concentrating on my breathing, or because I really can't control it anyway and my body likes to randomly torture me, a "Hummph" slips out.

Then another.

Right on cue, laughing behind me.

I hear a "hummph, hummph" like a mocking echo. Then a second voice. "Hummph." Giggling again.

Willa whips her head around.

"Shhhhhhh," she says.

"Whatever, Willard," Brooklyn says.

Miss Watson is returning to her seat and glances over with a stern expression.

Lee, who is on the other side of Willa, whispers something to her and everyone is quiet again. Except me, of course. "Hummph." It would be funny if it wasn't so nightmarish.

Rose goes back to the microphone.

"Following up on Miss Watson's point, we want our whole village to look spiffy too. Even if it's not on camera, lots of people will be coming in for the filming, and then of course after that we hope to see a surge in tourist traffic from those who saw the show. The village has made some improvements you may have noticed, new flowers and the like. If you could each do your part to make sure your lawns are mowed and looking tidy that would be most appreciated."

"Now to the guests — who were chosen by the show, not me. First will be yours truly, then as our one non-local, there will be a scientist coming from Environment Canada to talk about the Bay of Fundy and our tides. Les McLeod from Sea Kayak Adventures will be talking about what fun visitors can have exploring our shoreline. Em Gillis, our resident textile artist, will be next."

Wow, she's good at keeping a secret! She didn't even hint when I was there this afternoon.

"Mary of Mary's Catering will be making some of her delicious lobster chowder and sharing the recipe. And finally, Tyson Crowley will finish out the show as the musical guest.

"So, that's it!" she says. "And since it's so hot in here, anyone who doesn't have any questions can feel free to head out."

There's instantly the loud screech of about a hundred chairs being pushed back. The room fills with excited chatter.

Lee and Mom get up and turn to Willa and me.

"So, do you think we should go to the filming on Monday?" Mom asks. She winks at Lee.

"Probably," Willa says, and smiles.

"Yeah," I say. "I guess so, I mean, we may as well."

Chapter 8

The crowd quickly clears from the school parking lot. Mom and Lee walk back to The Inn together to chat and hang out. Willa and I are going for an ice-cream cone at Frosty Point Light, then we're heading to the beach. We're barely on the sidewalk before Brooklyn calls out to me. She and Madison are following right behind us.

"Hey, Hickory Dickory, what time is it? I've got to be home by nine."

I pretend not to hear her and keep on walking.

"Come on, I heard you in there. Tick, tick, tick, tick. Tick, tock. Tick, tock goes the clock. So what time is it?"

"Yeah, Hickory Dickory. I was surprised to hear you in there. I thought you'd given up your time-keeping hobby a long time ago," says Madison.

Hobby, yeah. That's it.

"I think it's nine now," I say to Willa, but loud

enough that Brooklyn and Madison can hear. "Too bad they can't stay out late like the big kids."

Willa laughs. I think it's really about seven-thirty or so.

"Whatever," Brooklyn says. "Anyway, Hickory Dickory, you'd better practise holding your breath all weekend, because you're insane if you think they're going to let someone making as much noise as you sit anywhere near the front for the show filming."

"Hummph. Hummmph," Madison broadcasts like she's on a loudspeaker.

Then they turn and walk away in the direction of their houses. "Hummmph, hummph, hummph" fades into the distance.

So, I have a tic. Sometimes I do it a lot, sometimes a little; sometimes I don't even realize I'm doing it. For every one I hear, I've probably done a bunch of others I didn't notice. It's an involuntary tic, which means I can't control it. If I'm being specific, my tics are *vocal*, because I make a sound rather than do an action like blinking or kicking my leg or something. Over the years I know Mom has read and learned *a lot* about tics. I've seen her search Google again and again, checking terms like "persistent," "provisional" and "transient."

When I was younger I used to think of transient being like the word "transport" and tried to imagine my tics hopping on a transport truck and zooming away forever. But it's more like my tics go on vacation then come back again. Someday they may go for good, but obviously that day isn't today.

My tics started in grade one and lasted until March break that time. They were bad on and off in grade three and came back for a few months after Christmas of grade four. When they finally stopped then, I thought they were gone for good. No such luck. But this is the first time they've been back since.

I went to the doctor when the tics first started. She said the best thing was to try to ignore the tics. It was important that Mom or Dad or anyone else didn't make a big deal of them. They shouldn't tell me to try to stop it, or to try to do it less, or more quietly, or anything, because I can't. They shouldn't be annoyed about them. Ever.

Mom talked to my teacher and the teacher even talked to the class. Back then everyone was still only six or seven and we were reminded every day at school about being nice little mice, bears who care, birds with kind words, tiny fishes with good wishes, and all that cute stuff that is wonderful and important and generally seems like a fabulous idea at the time. Sharing and caring and being friendly to everyone was a big deal then. No one bothered me about the tics.

There were a few other people in my grade who had some odd personal glitches, like Jaden still sucked his thumb, and Cole had to either sit on an exercise ball or ride the brain bike so he could concentrate in class. Ava was allergic to latex and couldn't touch balloons or rubber bands. Lots of kids still accidentally wore clothes backwards or inside out without noticing until later. Back then everyone kind of rolled with it.

But by the middle of grade three, when Brooklyn and Madison's mean-girl genes kicked in, they didn't mind mentioning the tics to me every chance they got. And I don't think it was because they forgot they weren't supposed to. Then of course it was like this big cause-and-effect thing started happening — a self-fulfilling prophecy. I did turn into the ticking hand on a clock going around and around in a circle. The more they teased me, the more anxious I got about the tics being obvious, and then because of that, the more obviously and often I ticced.

That's the super-annoying thing about them and why I'm so sure I'm tic, tick, ticking like a time bomb now. The tics can get worse with both anxiety and excitement. Hummph, hummph hooray!

So the fact that we're moving explains the anxiety. (For now I can't even think about moving to where the whole population doesn't already know about my tics and know that they are supposed to ignore them! I think I'd rather just permanently wear a shirt with my tic FAQs printed on it than have to explain it all even once. Yeah, not only will I be the "new kid," but I'll be the new kid with a side order of tics. There's a winning combination.) And excitement? Well, *Rise and Shine Canada* is coming on Monday of course.

I did learn to calm myself a little by doing deep breathing, which sometimes helps, but there's still no way I can stop them completely. I didn't need Brooklyn planting the idea in my head that I might be too loud in the audience for the filming. There's no way I'm not going.

"Hey, Hope, forget them," Willa says. "You'll be fine."

"Forget who?"

"Good. Exactly."

I'm sure going to try. Really, considering everything, Brooklyn and Madison are pretty much at the bottom of my list of current worries.

At Frosty Point Light, Willa and I both order their specialty, a Lighthouse Cone. It's soft ice cream that's a twist of vanilla and cherry. They give you a huge serving to look like a tall striped lighthouse and put a yellow gumdrop on top for the light.

We walk across the public beach. The tide is out. The sun is starting to lower in the sky and the long stretches of wet rock are reflecting the light, glinting bright. There aren't many people around. A few tourists are walking at a distance, along the openings of the sea caves.

We sit and eat our ice cream. Willa points her dancer toes into a pencil and doodles in the sand. We talk about every single thing that was mentioned at the meeting — at least twice. Then Willa walks home the way we came, and I head down the beach alone.

I walk slowly. A cormorant is perched on top of a driftwood log that's sticking out of the water. A few gulls are floating on the waves, bobbing up and down. There's a breeze that ripples the beach grass. The sounds of the grass rustling, the lapping water on the shore, and my footsteps squishing over the sand are all I can hear. It seems perfect. Calm. I haven't ticced once the whole time I've been walking.

It's getting dark enough now that the tall lamppost on the beach at the back of our property is on
— a soft glow guiding me home. Instead of a street-
light, we have a shore light. Dad made it and in-
stalled it for us. It runs completely on solar power
and turns on automatically at night. It's cool though
because Dad also added a light switch so we can
turn it off if we ever want to just sit in the glow
of the moon. I think Dad probably has the recycled
soul of an inventor. Maybe in another life he in-
vented the refrigerator or the toilet or something. I
think he's who I inherited my creativity from.

I keep walking toward the lamppost. Because
the tide is out and because of the light, I can see my
sea glass. It looks different every time it's exposed.
Today my screens are mostly covered by sand with
only one long skinny section along an edge showing.
Some of my glass is at the surface. I count three
green, a blue, two white and a piece of pink from my
grandmother's candy dish. They are triangles and
polygons, edges slightly rounded, smoothing, not
sharp enough to cut anymore, but Mother Nature
isn't nearly done yet.

I was kind of thinking of gathering all the glass
up at the end of the summer and taking it with me,
no matter how far along it was. But I'm not sure.

It might be important to let her finish what she started. I could leave it the way it is and check next summer when we visit. I'd have to pretty much forget about it I guess. But I could. I think. Maybe. I'll see. I don't know.

It would be one more thing I have to leave behind.

Chapter 9

Days since summer vacation started: 28
Days until Likely Departure Date: 33
Days until The Point of No Return: 45

I'm dreaming that I'm running down the beach, trying to get home before the storm starts. There's no rain and no lightning but the thunder is loud and continuous. Rumbling, rumbling. It doesn't stop. Even when I wake up. Which is strange. But I was wrong; it isn't thunder I'm hearing, it's the sound of probably every lawn mower in St. David's running at once. It's crazy loud and all over the place and kind of angry sounding. I mean, we're talking what I imagine dinosaur roars sounded like. This would be the perfect time to use a word I learned last year in music class — cacophony. And Mrs. O'Neill certainly never used it as a compliment.

I look at the clock; it's only 8:45 a.m. Not only did everyone listen to Mayor Rose about spiffing things up, they're all doing it early before it gets too hot.

I get out of bed and see Em across the street mowing her side yard. Bobby McIsaac is mowing at Mrs. Wright's. (Which confirms my new theory that cancelling Christmas in July was likely Mayor Rose's idea and not Karly's.) Then there's a big bump against the side of our house. Mom is mowing too, and I know she's just hit the edge of the porch, ramming the front wheels of the machine into it trying to get every last blade of grass. I think you're supposed to use the Whippersnipper if you're that close to the house. But Mom doesn't have a lot of lawn-care experience. I miss Dad. And Jacob.

Speaking of him, I check and, sure enough, Jacob messaged me back. I sent him a multi-paragraph explanation all about *Rise and Shine Canada* last night.

"Hope, Coolest thing ever! What are the chances? Even Dylan already texted me about it and you know how he calls St. David's St. Dullvid's. I wish I was there to see it live. We don't have a TV here at base camp, but I think I can watch online. Try to get on TV if you can. Make a really good poster and wave it around like a wild person. That was how Adam got shown at the curling championships. Gotta go! Trees need planting. Your FBF"

So, FBF isn't a typo of BFF; it stands for "Favourite Brother Forever," which Jacob made up. But Dylan and Adam are Jacob's BFFs. The fact that Adam was shown on TV in the audience when the World Curling Championships were held in Saint John a few years ago has been his claim to fame ever since. You could only see him for maybe two seconds, but it was still a big deal. *Rise and Shine Canada* is a big deal times a hundred. Maybe in other places, like in big cities, filming live TV shows happens a lot and is totally whatever, but not here. Plus, this is about us — about St. David's. We have the starring role.

I get dressed, go downstairs, and grab some cereal and orange juice. I hear the back door swing open.

"I'm in the kitchen, Mom," I call.

But Karly walks in. The morning sun hitting her bedazzled jacket lapels blinds me. She's wearing the same outfit as in the pictures on her car. Oh yes, she has her huge head and shoulders on both front doors and her hair kind of flows onto the back doors. The Karly-mobile is a little powder-blue Beetle. She has custom giant eyelashes on the front headlights that make them look like big bug eyes.

"Good morning, Hope. Your mom will be in

soon. She told me to head on in. We've got a show-ing this morning!" Karly smiles, obviously excited. She sets down a box filled with several vases of flow-ers, some scented candles, a bottle of Windex and a roll of paper towels. "It's great you're up. They'll be here in half an hour."

I nod and keep chewing my cereal.

"Don't mind me," she says. She lifts out a vase of flowers and sets it in the middle of the kitchen table.

"Hummph."

"Bless you," Karly says.

I take my cereal and juice and go to my room.

"Be sure to make your bed and bring those dish-es back down," Karly calls after me.

I hate the thought of strangers nosing around my room. But it's not because I figure they won't be impressed. My room is a beautiful turquoise, and the little vases I have filled with sea glass on the window ledge shine oceany bubbles on the walls when the sun passes through them. I have a fan-cy antique mirror with a huge scrolled frame that Mom spray-painted silver. The letters that spell out "Dream" above my bed are silver too. I have two blue beanbag chairs that are like puddles you can jump right into.

But until the house is sold, the room is all mine

and it's private. I don't want people to have an opinion about it. I don't need to think about people saying, "Well, I suppose this could be the dog's room," or something.

If I wasn't such a respectable old soul and this wasn't real life but an episode of a TV comedy, I'd probably find a way to sabotage the showing. You know, like let a squirrel (or ten) loose in my room. Plug and overflow both upstairs toilets. Leave rotting dead fish here and there in cabinets and drawers. (Not even Karly's cranberry-orange-twist candle could cancel out that stench.)

But I know Mom and Dad worry about the house not selling. And not-selling doesn't mean not-moving. It means they would stress about someone having to take care of it here while we are far away in Toronto. No hilarious hijinks on my part are going to help my cause.

Deep inside, I'm really not feeling mature and fine with it, but I guess there's nothing I can do. I make my bed as neatly as I can.

Mom leans in my bedroom door. "I'm sorry if Karly surprised you, but I figured you'd be up. She texted me last minute about the showing. Do you want to eat breakfast down at The Inn?"

"Sure," I say. I didn't eat any more of my cereal

after I came upstairs. "And Mom, did Karly say who the people were?"

"An older couple from Saint John, looking for a summer place."

"So, no kids? No family?"

Mom shakes her head.

"And they wouldn't even live here year-round?"

"I don't know, sweetie. I don't think so though." She seems like she might add something else but doesn't.

I nod. I look around the room, then focus on my sea glass on the window ledge.

"I'd like to see it go to a family too," Mom says, "but we can't choose our buyers. And I think the chance of the house selling to the very first people who look at it is pretty small anyway."

"Yeah." I nod. "Okay."

"Meet you out on the porch in five minutes," she says.

I sit for a bit, then get off my bed and loosen the covers, swirling them into a ball. I knock my pillow onto the floor. I leave my cereal bowl and juice on my desk. I tilt my mirror crooked. As a finishing touch, I pull open two dresser drawers and randomly toss three T-shirts, letting them stay where they land. It's not sabotage; it's a protest. Just this one time. See, Karly, I can stage the house too. I close my bedroom door behind me.

As Mom and I walk up to The Inn, Willa's dad waves at us from his ride-on mower. We eat breakfast, and when Willa and I leave for the library, he's still out there finishing up near the sidewalk.

There are lots of people already making posters when we get there — a bunch of high school girls and two little kids with their mother. Thankfully, there's no Brooklyn or Madison.

I really like making posters, but I think I'm much better at coming up with ideas and slogans than I am at the drawing part. Last year I won second place in a drug awareness poster contest. My poster said "Slugs don't do drugs. They're smarter than you think!" Which I figured was super clever and hilarious considering slugs are the dumbest creatures alive. First place was a poster with the generic line "Hugs are better than drugs," which I'm sure has already been used 1.3 million times. But it had a picture of a cute pair of owls hugging with their wings. I have no idea why; I haven't heard of owls being big drug users.

Anyway, according to Willa, who told me in the most good-natured, sweet way, my brown slugs looked like pieces of poop with antennae. That was obviously the problem. I think the abstract patterns of quilting are a much better match for my creativity.

Today's poster is going to be words only. That will look better on TV. I choose a sheet of orange bristol board. I print "The Sun Rises in the EAST!" in big letters with a thick black marker, then add some gold glitter around the outside. Miss Watson says it looks great, and I have to say I agree. Willa uses a sheet of neon-pink bristol board and prints "Hey, Anne, I'm a Fan!" She goes wild with the glitter and covers every letter, alternating between silver and gold. I imagine it will look awesome in the bright morning sun — like disco ball sparkly. Miss Watson gushes about it, and I bet if Karly saw it she would too.

Willa has to leave for a highland dance competition and doesn't expect to be back until way after supper. We make plans to meet tomorrow to figure out the details of our arrival at the filming on Monday morning. I head back home and Mom is already there, sitting on the porch reading.

"Karly said they thought the place was too big for what they needed," Mom says.

"Oh yeah," I say. I wonder what they thought of my room. "Did Karly say anything else?"

"Just that she wishes she priced it higher." Mom smiles and shakes her head. "She thinks we'll have a lot of interest after the show airs Monday."

I go inside. The house smells like a mix of vanilla and something fruity. In my room, my bed is made and my pillow is perfectly propped against the headboard. The dishes are gone, the mirror is straightened and the clothes are back in the drawers. Karly even left one of the vases of flowers on my dresser. Oh well. I don't know how I'll feel when the next showing comes along, but hopefully it will be better.

Chapter 10

Days since summer vacation started: 29
Days until Likely Departure Date: 32
Days until The Point of No Return: 44

Mom's sitting at the kitchen table with her laptop open, video chatting with Dad, when I come downstairs in the morning. She doesn't notice me so I hang out in the doorway and listen for a minute. Mom is telling him my tics came back. She's a little worried. The volume isn't turned up enough that I can hear what Dad says. "It's going to be such a huge adjustment." Mom pauses. Dad says something else and then Mom says, "The doctor? I suppose it's a possibility but I don't want to upset her more by making a big deal of it." I take that as my cue to enter before Dad convinces her to send me. I don't want to waste any of my precious last summer in St. David's going to doctor's appointments.

"Good morning, Daddy!" I yell loudly.

"Hope!" he says, and I walk around beside Mom so he can see me. "I miss you. I can't wait until you come up here."

"Miss you too," I say. I hadn't really forgotten about my visit to Toronto coming up, but I've been trying so hard to just focus on *Rise and Shine Canada* that I haven't been thinking about it at all.

"Did Mom tell you what's happening tomorrow?" I ask.

"She did. I'm going to record it and watch for a peek of you in the audience. Out of all the places they could choose, eh? I'm so glad you're still there to see it."

We talk a bit longer. He seems happy. I try not to notice the totally beige and boring wall and tiny kitchen in the apartment he's staying in. Mom wants to talk to him after I'm done. I get some cereal and eat it in the living room. I don't purposely listen anymore, but when Mom lowers her voice, I do strain a bit to hear her since it must be something important. I hear her almost whisper, "What about Plan C?"

I wonder if it could have to do with my tics, but if the doctor is Plan A and that hopefully isn't happening, there's no way they've already jumped over Plan B and right to Plan C. It's probably something to do with selling the house, I guess. Probably some new strategy Karly came up with.

After lunch, I go to Em's. There are three cars parked in her small lot, and when I step inside, there are eight people in her gallery. Em is behind the counter, with Stitches sitting front and centre. I wave and point to the studio. Em nods and smiles.

I go to my work area. My quilt for Willa is on the design wall. Em ironed all my seams for me and put it back up. I just have to add the sand and sea glass section that goes below the ocean part. I dig through Em's scrap bin looking for fabric bits to be sea glass and rocks. I'll have maybe five or six sea glass pieces in different colours — a green and a blue and for sure a deep yellowish gold to represent the smashed piggy bank pieces Willa gave me. I choose beige and brown pieces for the sand, and a couple of greys for sections of rocks.

After I've picked out all my fabrics, I start "auditioning" them (that's what Em calls it) on the design wall. I arrange pieces to see how they look together. I change my mind about some and add in others. I move bits around and around. Em is busy in the gallery and I manage to not only make my final choices but cut several pieces of fabric to the size I need before she comes in.

"You're a natural talent, Hope," she says, looking at what I have so far. "Sorry I was so long. It's been busy this afternoon. But can I get you to help me with something before you finish sewing that up?"

"Sure," I say. I figure it's going to be addressing a few packages, which I don't mind doing.

She leaves, then comes back with a stack of four quilts. Even with them folded I can tell they're colourful and gorgeous, the same as everything she makes.

"These are the ones I'm taking to the show tomorrow," she says. "And the village is buying one as a gift for Anne. Which one should it be? I'll go with whatever you pick."

"Hummph. Hummph." Deep breath. "Really? Are you sure?" I ask.

"Absolutely."

My mind zaps out simultaneous signals for both excitement and anxiety; I feel the tingle of them travel from my brain to my belly. I try to think if I know anything about Anne, other than her being a host of the show. No. I wonder what her favourite colour is. Should I Google it? Does she like fancy things? Simpler things?

Em's unfolded the quilts on a table. They are all

so different. I could randomly eliminate them one by one. But then, Em could have done that herself.

"If it helps, Rose said she wanted a nice souvenir representing our village. She's giving Phil a painting of the sea caves. So if there's a quilt there that somehow seems more familiar to you, I guess, than the others, that would be a good choice."

"Thanks, I think it does help." And that's exactly how I choose. Em told me once that good art should give you a feeling, like make you think or experience something, even if you don't know why. Nature and the outdoors can do that too — being in certain surroundings. Places can have a special meaning. Objects that remind you of a place can be meaningful. Which of these quilts would give Anne the special feeling of remembering this place?

"This one," I say. "For sure." I choose one that has probably a hundred or more tiny scraps of all colours pieced into the middle close together, then a huge section of warm sunshiny yellow all around the outside.

"Then this one it is," Em says. "I'll see you tomorrow, I imagine?"

"Wouldn't miss it," I say.

🐚 🐚 🐚

From the widow's walk, Willa and I can see three large trucks in the public beach parking lot. Nothing is unloaded yet but several men are walking along the shore and marking sections with stakes. There are two cars from a security company in the lot too. One is parked across the entryway. A man is leaning against the hood.

Willa said she heard the filming mentioned on the radio when she was coming back from her dance competition. (She was the overall winner for her class, as usual.) People from outside of the village will absolutely be coming. Willa also said about twenty people called The Inn wanting to reserve a room for tonight so they'd already be here early in the morning, but The Inn was fully booked. I bet there's a giant crowd tomorrow.

"Do you think going at 4:00 a.m. will be early enough?" Willa asks. Her competitive spirit has kicked in and I know she'll settle for nothing less than the front row. She's as excited about the show as I am, even though it's not as a distraction from imminent life relocation and wrecking.

"I hope so," I say. "I figure it should be."

"I hope so too. I'm sure we'll get in, but I really want great seats. Anyway, that's the earliest Mom will let me go. And she already thinks that's crazy."

"It's good crazy though," I say.

"The best," Willa says.

We go over all our details for the morning. We both have to set our PVRs to record the show. We will both set our alarm clocks, tablet alarms and stove timers to be sure we wake up. I'll meet Willa outside The Inn at 3:50 a.m. If either of us is late, we'll call the other. We're both going to wear blue shirts because Willa read online that's a good colour to wear on TV.

We say goodnight to each other even though it's only 8:00 p.m. The chances of either of us falling asleep any time soon are slim to none, but the sooner we go to bed, the sooner morning comes.

Chapter 11

Days since summer vacation started: 30
Days until Likely Departure Date: 31
Days until The Point of No Return: 43

It's super weird to be walking down the sidewalk in the dark. When I slipped out the back door of the house, I could see our shore light down at the beach, but up here it's pitch black. It seems more like late at night than early in the morning. There are no cars driving by, no birds singing, no lights on in anyone's houses. (Even Mom is still asleep at our place and only going to the filming at 6:00 a.m.)

It's almost a little spooky. I walk faster. I thought for sure the village had more street lights.

Then suddenly someone is running up the sidewalk toward me, holding what looks like a baseball bat. I take in a breath to scream, but at the exact same second I realize the person isn't really running but gracefully springing forward.

It's Willa with her rolled-up poster.

"I didn't want to wait at The Inn. It was too hard to just stand there," she says, as she rushes up to me. "Let's go!"

We hurry down to the beach, and there's no sign of anyone anywhere so it looks like we might be first. But when we round the slight turn and go past Frosty Point Light to the parking lot, we can see nine or ten people already gathered.

"Rats," Willa says.

And yeah, it is kind of disappointing — especially when I see who's first in line.

"Hey, Willard," Brooklyn calls. "You'd think that hanging around with Hickory Dickory, you'd at least get here on time. Did you forget to set her alarm?"

Madison laughs.

Willa looks at me and I roll my eyes. Brooklyn's mean, but I will admit she's also kind of clever.

At 6:00 a.m., when they start to let people in, the line reaches across the parking lot and winds down the road. Brooklyn and Madison run and take the two seats in the very middle of the front row. Rather than sit right beside them, Willa and I leave two seats and sit slightly to the right. Everyone files in and the audience area starts to fill up.

Jacob's friends Dylan and Adam sit at the end of the second row. Not far down from them and almost directly behind us are Mayor Rose's husband and Miss Watson. Mom and Lee eventually come in and end up near the back. There's a lot of chatter and excitement with the slight sound of waves and seagulls in the background. The sun is up and it's beautiful and bright.

The stage is about a classroom length away from us. It's smaller and not as high as I thought it would be. I mean, it's only raised about a foot off the beach. It's placed closer to the water than our seats are, so the ocean is in the background. It's odd but I realize they moved the stage from where we saw it set up when we were looking down from the widow's walk yesterday — like a last-minute change. I guess maybe it seems more scenic this way. The caves are off to the left. The tide is out so they are completely uncovered.

On the stage are two tall stools on one side and three chairs set behind a low coffee table on the other. There are four large cameras on tall stands — one set back a little bit from each end of the stage, one behind the stage pointing at the audience and one in the front middle of the stage.

I'm glad we're sitting a bit off to one side so

the middle camera isn't right in our way. There's a microphone on a long swinging arm and a TV monitor and other bits of equipment all over the place. A seagull is perched on a tall speaker stand. It's like he's ready to watch the show too. People wearing headsets are going back and forth checking things.

There's so much to take in and keep track of that Willa and I barely talk after we sit down. When a man finally stands in front of the crowd to make some announcements before the show starts, Willa reaches over and squeezes my hand.

"Here we go," I whisper.

"Good morning, St. David's, New Brunswick!" the man calls.

There's applause and cheering.

"Excellent," he says. "That's exactly the response we're looking for. My name is Eric, and I'm a producer here on *Rise and Shine Canada*. I'd like to thank you on behalf of all of us for joining our filming today!"

Then he explains a whole bunch of stuff that everyone seems to pay close attention to. He reminds us the show is live. They will definitely have shots of the audience included so look enthusiastic. Some parts of the show we won't see, like the news and weather reports coming from the main studio in Toronto. Also, we won't see the commercials or the clips of the village they filmed earlier, which will be shown before and after each break. He asks everyone to stay quiet during the actual interviews.

When he says this, Brooklyn leans ahead and raises her finger to her lips. "Shhhhh," she whispers in my direction. I ignore her. Nothing is going to wreck this.

"Now," Eric says, and looks at his watch. "Filming starts in five minutes. St. David's, New Brunswick, allow me to introduce you to the rest of Canada. Here's to a great show everyone!"

He walks away and Anne and Phil step onto the stage. Anne is wearing a pretty purple wrap around blouse with a long tie that hangs down over her white skirt. Phil is wearing a light blue shirt but no tie. They sit on the stools. A makeup person comes out and powders Anne's nose and forehead slightly, then smooths her bangs to one side. Both Anne and Phil are holding a stack of cue cards. They talk to each other, but no one in the audience can hear them yet.

Anne looks through her cards. Eric yells, "Three minutes!"

Everyone gets in place. Two minutes. One.

"Good morning, it's time to rise and shine, Canada!" Anne says. "I'm Anne McQuarrie."

"And I'm Phil Booker. As I'm sure you observant viewers — even those of you without your coffee yet — have noticed, we aren't in the studio this morning. We'll tell you why in just a second, but first we're going to let the fine folks of St. David's, New Brunswick, say good morning too."

That's our cue to cheer, and everyone goes wild. Willa and I wave our posters and yell "Wooooooooo" over and over. People at the back are clapping, whistling and yelling like us. I notice the woman with the camera that faces the audience pan it slowly back and forth. The cheering goes on until Eric makes a hand-lowering motion for us to stop.

"Wow!" Phil says. "That'll wake you up. Thank you, everyone."

"Now," Anne says. "As to why we're here. We're starting a new, special summer feature. Today is our first stop in a week of travels to what we're calling Canada's Tiniest Treasures. Each day we'll be on location in a different village that many of you may not have heard of, but which is a lovely little spot that we think you should know more about. In each place you'll meet local guests and learn more about these wonderful communities.

We are travelling east to west, so that's why we're starting here today."

"And," Phil says, "as you know, we love to have contests on *Rise and Shine Canada*, so there's a little part of this special week that you'll all be able to participate in. We're announcing it now so you can be sure to pay extra attention to the show each day."

Willa looks at me and raises her eyebrows. I shrug. Maybe they're giving away some plane tickets or something so a lucky viewer can visit one of the villages.

"One of these places will be voted on by you at home to be our ultimate Canadian tiny treasure. The contest will open next week after we've visited everywhere. We'll announce how the online contest will work on Friday, which will also give participating villages a chance to convince you they're the best choice, with content they can upload to our website. We think it will be a lot of fun. Aaaaand, of course we have a fabulous prize for the whole winning community to enjoy. Which," he pauses, "you'll find out about on Friday too."

The cheering is even louder than last time. The contest is for the village. I wonder what the prize is. At school, whenever it's a prize for everyone, it's always a big pizza-and-ice-cream party. I wonder if

I dare dream for a huge village party — and soon, before I leave. One thing I do know is that Willa will want to win, guaranteed.

As if on cue she pivots in her chair and gives me two thumbs up.

Again Eric has to signal for us to quiet down.

Oh, I hope the show goes well.

But of course it will.

Chapter 12

Anne and Phil throw it back to the studio for news and weather. In the meantime they move behind the coffee table. Mayor Rose comes out and sits with them. Her face is red.

As soon as the filming starts again, I figure out it's because she's nervous. She seems to pause a long time before answering their questions and then giggles at the end of each one. She takes a big drink from her glass of water. It seems to relax her a bit for the next few questions but then at the end of the interview, Phil asks her what is one thing people should definitely do if they visit here this summer. She says, and I quote, "Swim in our beautiful Bay of Funny." *Funny*, she says! Then she does the nervous giggle again and because of that you can tell Anne and Phil wonder if it's supposed to be a joke.

Rose doesn't seem to realize what she actually said. There's an awkward pause, which doesn't happen much on TV. Two seconds feels like two years. Rose stands up and I know the cameraman isn't expecting it because her face disappears off the top of the monitor. Then her headless body gestures widely. Her arms swing way out.

"Our beautiful Bay of Fundy, the Atlantic Ocean, here, all around us," Rose says. I turn around and peek at her husband behind us. He's smiling — proud of her. Who cares if it wasn't perfect?

"Oh yes, definitely," Phil says, looking relieved. He motions to Rose to sit back down. She does. "Thank you so much, Rose Riley, mayor of St. David's."

The camera pans across the water. I look out. It is beautiful. The tide is coming in. Waves are gently lapping at the distant shore. The gull that's still perched on the speaker squawks as if he knows it's the perfect time to add a seaside sound effect. Hopefully everyone at home is noticing. And giving us points for that — if they're keeping some sort of score to decide who to vote for.

After the commercial break is Les from Sea Kayak Adventures. He doesn't seem nervous at all. He talks about some things you can explore along the shore while kayaking, including the sea caves. He also talks about a special sunset tour he leads himself, and the way he describes it makes it sound like something you'd put on your bucket list for sure.

Mary of Mary's Catering is next with her lobster chowder. She has a giant steaming pot and ladles two generous bowlfuls for Anne and Phil to try. Huge chunks of lobster stick out of the broth. Anne tries hers first and claims it is absolutely delicious. Best she's had — anywhere. Mary blushes. I add some points to our village's total.

"Well, that's high praise," Phil says. "But let's see what the real expert here thinks."

Mary picks up Phil's bowl to pass it to him. A full claw of lobster meat sits on top near the spoon. It looks super yummy.

Which, unfortunately, the seagull must think too.

The big white bird suddenly swoops down, beak wide open, zeroing in on the lobster chunk. Mary sees the gull coming and tries to swat it away, but instead she knocks Phil's bowl out of her other hand. The seagull gulps the loose lobster piece in mid-air as the chowder sprays everywhere. Most of the hot broth splatters all over Phil's arm.

He swears.

And there is no beeping sound over top of the

bad word. He winces, squeezes his eyes shut super tight, and shakes his arm several times.

Anne is aghast. Mary is aghast.

"Oh my soul, oh my goodness," Mary says, and raises her hand to her heart. She instantly turns the same colour grey as the pot the chowder's in. Great. Automatic deduction for attacking one of the hosts with hot chowder: at least 5 to 100 points on any scale. I wonder if Phil's arm is burned.

Willa turns to me and opens her eyes wide. I mouth, "I know!"

"I'm so, so sorry," Mary says, but Phil stops her. He has composed himself. He squeezes the excess chowder out of his sleeve, then rolls it up.

"No worries," he says. "All good now. It seems that bird just wanted an audition at being the show mascot."

Mary doesn't say anything. She seems super distracted, staring at Phil's arm as if she's waiting for a flaming-red rash to appear on it.

"At least we know the chowder is seagull approved," Phil goes on and laughs.

Anne laughs too. Mary doesn't.

So, obviously that part of the show could have gone way better. I certainly wasn't expecting this morning's taping to have its own blooper reel. And

I'm sure the clip of the sneaky seagull will end up on YouTube. It screams viral video. But as I hear Eric joke to Phil while the show has been thrown back to Toronto for another news and weather update, "Hey, anything can happen on live TV."

Phil rushes off to change his shirt and then somehow the show is already half over! The man from Environment Canada is next. He talks about the Bay of Fundy tides and how they are the highest in the world. It seems a bit like a boring science lesson, but maybe if you aren't from here and haven't already heard it all, it's interesting. He talks about how tide charts and calculations go into planning all kinds of things along the coast. As an example, he explains that he's sure the producers took the tide into consideration when placing the set-up here today. Phil and Anne nod along, but I can't help but notice Eric glance out to the water. The waves are getting closer to the back of the stage — not too close, but closer for sure. I remember how the position of the stage was changed from yesterday.

Finally it is Em's turn. During the commercial break she carries in her stack of four quilts and sets them on the coffee table. She looks like a supermodel as usual, and I can hear a few whispers in the crowd. She's wearing a green dress. She sits on a chair on one side of the coffee table, and Anne and Phil stay on the other. Em looks out at the crowd and waves when she sees me in the front row. I smile and make a clapping motion with my hands without actually making any sound.

About thirty seconds into Em's conversation with Anne and Phil it's obvious she's the star of the show. She smiles as she talks and sounds both super friendly and super smart at the same time. This has to be making people forget about the chowder attack. Her quilts look beautiful in the early morning sun. Anne gushes over them. She even points out the one that I know she is getting as her favourite. Total score! Bonus points for me.

Phil keeps smiling at Em and volunteers himself as her "personal clothesline," holding up the quilts one by one with both arms outstretched, completely blocking himself, while she and Anne admire the details. Anne jokes and peeks behind one quilt like it's a curtain and asks him how he's holding up. Some people in the audience laugh.

Then at the end of the segment when Mayor Rose comes out to give the quilt to Anne, she is so thrilled she hugs both Rose and Em. Rose seems calmer now and jokes with Phil not to worry because they have a gift for him too. "And it's nothing you'll have to compete with a seagull for," she adds, and winks. Anne giggles. This is all going much, much better. We are really ending strong.

The final part of the show will be Tyson Crowley performing. Eric makes an announcement to remind us to cheer every bit as loud at the end as we did at the beginning. There will be lots of audience shots again. He starts to say something else, but then he puts his hand to his headset and listens. Whatever message he gets sends him running around to the back of the stage. As he does I can see the slightest splash of water. The tide has made its way in. They shouldn't have moved the stage. It would have been fine where it was yesterday — nowhere near the water.

"They should've listened." Rose's husband is talking to Miss Watson behind me. "We told them I don't know how many times not to move that stage. We said they were gambling with the tide. But no, no, they figured they could beat it, get the show done first, and the waves would hold off like rain or something. Honestly." I turn slightly and see him shaking his head. "Couldn't leave well enough alone — claimed they had to move it to get the sun just so in the background."

Other people start to notice the water too. I elbow

Willa. There's whispering in the crowd. We had all been so entranced watching the filming, the ocean sneaked up on us. But at least it's still just barely there. The waves lap up to the edge of the stage and stop. They aren't crashing into it. And the stage is a foot up. No one is going to get swept away. Eric talks to the cameraman at the side of the stage. The show is so close to being over. I see the cameraman look at his watch. They laugh and shrug. They don't seem concerned. Good thing. I mean, we certainly don't need the show to end with the whole stage floating out to sea. Eric says something into his headset, and six crew members emerge from the trucks parked along the beach edge. I bet we're about to see the quickest teardown in history once Anne and Phil say goodbye.

Although the other guests entered from the back of the stage, Tyson is led around to the front. He takes his place behind a microphone stand. He adjusts his guitar strap slightly, then runs his hand through his hair. He waves to someone in the crowd. Anne and Phil hover off to his left side. Eric gives the countdown signal that filming will be starting again. Phil introduces Tyson, and we cheer and cheer. He begins to strum his guitar. Anne and Phil slowly back out of view of the camera.

Tyson starts to sing. Phil takes a few more steps backwards without paying enough attention and slips on a little patch of the stage that's wet from the spray of a wave. At first it seems like he'll catch himself, but then his other foot starts to go out from under him and he instinctively grabs at a nearby speaker on a tall stand to save himself from falling. It's not a good choice. Oh no, no, no. In fact, it is a very, very, very bad idea.

The speaker can't take Phil's weight and it's suddenly "Timber!" as it falls directly backwards off the stage. Into the edge of the ocean. Phil too. But instead of a splash there is a sort of mini explosion as electronics and water don't mix and something is shorted out. Tyson pivots around immediately, unsure what to do, but amazingly keeps on singing. I can see his lips moving even though his microphone has gone quiet. Anne screams, and it turns out her mic is still working, so it is broadcast as horror-movie loud. Phil gets back up, soaking wet. His hair is no longer slicked in place. It is dripping. He picks a piece of seaweed off his shirt and flings it backwards like an angry merman. Crew members start to rush in different directions. Some splash and slip in the water.

Because of the disaster happening onstage, a

camerawoman immediately pivots her camera to the audience. I'm not sure our reactions make for must-see TV. I don't want to think how we look. It's probably something like — no, no, I really don't want to think of it.

"Hummph, hummph, hummph."

I put my poster in front of my face when my tics start, but considering the situation I guarantee not a single person notices me in the slightest.

Chapter 13

Willa and I head to The Inn to play back her recording of the show. I'm not feeling anywhere near as keen as I figured I would be. My excitement kind of washed away as soon as the tide decided to make its TV debut. But we'll see. You know that expression "the magic of television"? Well, that's what I'm hoping for. *Abracadabra, one, two, three, poof!* and it miraculously doesn't seem as disastrous onscreen as it did live.

We sit on the couch in her den and start the show. It's so weird. Instant déjà vu, right? There are miniature Anne and Phil, just them up close without any of the rest of the stage or all the equipment around them. With the angle of the camera, you can see part of the sea caves and lots of the ocean. Anne's purple blouse makes the water look sapphire blue. Then the next thing you know, Willa and I are on the screen. Like the first ones out of the whole audience!

"Hope, look!" Willa says.

The camera seems to hold on us as we cheer and hold our signs high, then it pans down the front row past Brooklyn and Madison and back through the audience. Wow, there are a lot of people. I even see Lee and Mom for a split second.

"It looks amazing," Willa says.

I agree.

Maybe, just maybe, the rest will look amazing too.

Like the producer said, before each commercial break they show photos of the village. They play music in the background, and across the bottom of the screen it says "St. David's, New Brunswick" on one line and "Visiting Canada's Tiniest Treasures" with a little picture of a treasure chest filled with gold below it. There are photos of the sea caves, a long shot of the beach with kayaks in the water, lots and lots of buildings and older houses, a near-by lighthouse, even a close-up of the flowers shaped like a lobster.

Mayor Rose's segment comes on and it isn't too bad. Nothing is magically transformed, and she still appears to decapitate herself when she stands up unexpectedly, but you only see her for a split second before the camera switches to Anne and Phil.

Unfortunately, Mary and the seagull situation appear about a million times worse. Mainly because you can't see the seagull at all. (So at least that's a negative on the viral video.) He must be flying just above what the camera is showing onscreen. So it looks like Mary swats at Phil's bowl of chowder on purpose and for no good reason! It's a random attack, like her arm is possessed by an evil spirit. And there is still no beep over Phil's swear word.

"Oh, that is so not good," Willa says.

Tell me about it. If there's any magic at work, I'm pretty sure it's a curse.

Willa fast-forwards through the Environment Canada guy. We watch Em and she's a total pro. Then Willa fast-forwards again through the last news and weather. All that's left in the show will be Tyson performing.

"Cross your fingers," Willa says.

She lets the show play and we should look away, but we can't. It is exactly as bad as I remember. Or maybe worse because they keep switching camera angles, probably hoping to show something normal, but that makes it look more like the entire production is a wreck. The only thing that's different is that after Anne screams, you don't see or hear anything live anymore. The same pictures of St. David's from earlier are shown again until the credits roll.

I look at Willa. I know neither of us is sure what to say. You only get one chance to make a first impression, and that was the first impression our village made on national TV.

"Well," Willa finally says. "So it wasn't perfect, sure. But nothing says the other places are going to do any better."

Really? I know Willa likes to stay positive, but I'm thinking that the only way tomorrow's show (wherever it is) could be worse is if a sinkhole opens up and swallows the whole stage, or Phil jumps on the coffee table mid-interview, rips open his shirt, transforms into a werewolf and then wildly rampages through the audience.

"Besides, we still get to add things to the website next week to help us out. And you know that if it comes down to voting online it's not who did the best on TV, but whoever can get the most people to actually vote for them."

I nod. She is right about that. It does come down to the voting — so, maybe? Yeah, sure, maybe. If I have to move, at least it would be cool to go to the best going-away party ever first.

Chapter 14

Days since summer vacation started: 31
Days until Likely Departure Date: 30
Days until The Point of No Return: 42

I'll admit to being curious, so I watch *Rise and Shine Canada* the rest of the week. I record it so I can fast-forward through the news, weather, commercials and boring parts. It makes the show go by super quick.

On Tuesday's *Rise and Shine Canada*, Anne and Phil are in a village called Atkinson. It's in Ontario, right on the border with Quebec.

Anne and Phil are safely sitting on the wide front steps of the old stone town hall — no ocean anywhere in sight. Anne is wearing a red dress that perfectly matches the bouquet of roses set on a small table between them. It's a sunny day. There's a big crowd, although not as many people have posters like we did.

The mayor is their first guest, just like Mayor Rose was here. Then they welcome a local historian and the head of a regional theatre troupe. The owner of a bakery called Fun with Buns comes on and serves these delicious-looking maple croissants. No birds fly in to try to snatch them away. Phil doesn't get hit, or burned, or spilled on. He doesn't drop so much as a crumb. The musical guest sings beautifully. Then I realize there's only one guest left even though there's still half an hour of the show to go. Heading into the commercials, they show photos of many historic stone and brick buildings.

When they come back, Anne and Phil have moved to an empty parking lot. They're standing in front of a hockey net. The crowd has moved too and are already cheering and whistling. I imagine Eric gives them the signal to quiet down.

"And now," Phil says, "a little trivia question for you at home. Do you know what tiny town hockey legend Joel Power is from?"

I don't even pay any attention to hockey and I know exactly who Joel Power is. He's the man walking across the TV screen now. The audience is clapping, yelling and whistling. So, I guess Atkinson is his hometown. Convenient for them. I don't need to see the end of the show. I'm sure there will be some shootout with Joel and Phil and maybe audience members. Perhaps a full-on road hockey game will break out. Well played, Atkinson. Well played.

I heard a little *ding* while I was watching TV so I check and I have a message from Jacob. The first thing he sent is a picture of a clown wearing a bathing suit and a giant rubber duck floaty. At the top it says, "Where is a clown's favourite place to swim?" What? I have no idea what this has to do with anything and I kind of wonder if he meant to send it to someone else. I scroll down to see what's written at the bottom. It says, "In the Bay of Funny, of course!" Great. I feel my eyes roll. That's one meme I won't be sharing.

Then below it is an old music video. Without even clicking it I can see it's for a song called "The Tide is High." Oh, Jacob is hilarious. He obviously got a chance to see yesterday's show. I scroll past about twenty-five of those smileys that are laughing so hard they're crying to get to his message. "Just kidding! The show was awesome! Best thing ever. All the stuff that went wrong just made it more fun to watch. I saw you — great poster! Gotta go. We are moving camp and going off grid so I won't be in touch until next week. Your FBF, Jacob."

All the stuff that went wrong. Lovely. So it was

certainly obvious there were problems even if you weren't here to witness it live. And Atkinson's show today went wonderfully. Perfectly. Oh well. I guess all I can do is hope for the best (or worst?) for the rest of the week.

Wednesday's show comes from a village in Saskatchewan called Dew Lake. Anne and Phil are in a high-school gym because the weather didn't cooperate and it's pouring rain. But a little rain isn't anything compared to high tide. Once again the format is about the same as the shows in the other two villages. They have six guests. The mayor is first. Then there's a man who owns an organic flour mill. After him is the owner of a local restaurant, who serves saskatoon berry pie to Anne and Phil — and the whole audience. They move on to a landscape photographer and a local children's author, and finally for the last guest they have a Ukrainian dance group perform.

On Thursday's *Rise and Shine Canada* they are in a place called Four Hills in Alberta's Badlands. Anne and Phil are set up in front of some cool-looking rocks they say are called hoodoos. After the mayor, a fossil expert comes on with some amazing dinosaur bones. Then the next guest is a tour guide who takes people out to see fossils and hike the Badlands. Keeping with the theme, a local candy company owner brings "dinosaur bones" for Anne and Phil to sample. Phil comments that the "bones" taste like jelly beans. The last two guests are a painter and a pianist. There's no question it was another good, disaster-free show. Oh well.

Tomorrow I won't get to watch because I'm flying to Toronto to see Dad.

Chapter 15

Days since summer vacation started: 34
Days until Likely Departure Date: 27
Days until The Point of No Return: 39

Mom and I leave early in the morning. We drive through St. David's and then along the coast of the Bay of Fundy. The beams of sun on the water glow across the tops of waves like gold ribbons. We turn and drive through the forest, through the country, then reach the city limits and the Saint John Airport.

I am flying as an "unaccompanied minor." It's a fancy way of saying I'm twelve and going by myself. The airline will keep track of me. It's like I'm an important package being shipped from Mom to Dad. Airmail. Special delivery. Maybe I can even get some "Fragile" stickers to put on my shirt. The airport attendant is very nice, chatting with Mom, explaining how they'll take such good care of me. Mom is nervous. I can tell because she keeps playing with her hair and running her hand back through it. I'm totally nervous too. More than a few tics have slipped out. I know people fly all the time, but it's still hard to think of being way, way up in the sky, just sitting there in a giant metal hot dog with wings. I'm taking slow, deep breaths and acting as calm as I can.

"Daddy will be right there at the other end. And if by any rare chance he's not, don't worry, he's just late and someone will wait with you. There's nothing to worry about at all. It'll be fun. Flying is fun. You'll love the view from the plane. And if it seems bumpy in the air at all, that's called turbulence, no need to worry. It happens sometimes. And if you have to pee, there's a—"

"I know, Mom," I say. She told me all this three times in the car.

"I just love you, girlie," she says, and squeezes me tight.

"You too. It'll all be good. See you Sunday."

The plane is smaller than I thought it would be. There are two seats on each side of the aisle. Mine is about halfway back, by a window. The flight isn't full so no one sits beside me.

When the plane starts moving it goes slowly

down to the end of the runway and it doesn't seem much different than driving in a car. Or that's what I'm telling myself anyway. We turn at the end and stop for a few seconds. My stomach starts swirling and it feels like my ribs are bobbing up and down. "Hummph. Hummph." Then the pilot seems to step on the gas and we go faster and faster until we start to lift off the ground. It's as if we're zooming up a steep, invisible hill, higher and higher. My ears feel funny. They pop. I swallow and they pop again. So, that actually wasn't that bad. My stomach settles down. We're in the air.

After a little while, the pilot announces we're at our "cruising altitude." It means that now we are high enough up we can fly in a flat, straight line. And we are way, way, way up, above where kites and birds and fog and even some clouds go. Looking down, I can cover whole lakes by putting my thumb on the window. I can hide a house under my pinky fingernail. Then as we continue to fly across New Brunswick, it's mostly trees and more trees. Eventually I lean back in my seat and close my eyes.

I can't wait to see Dad. And for now, as long as I think of going to the city as a fun summer trip and not Step One to Imminent Disaster, I have to admit I can be excited about that too.

We land safely, and just like Mom said he'd be, Dad is waiting. I run over and give him a hug. He kisses me on top of the head. As we walk toward the tunnel that leads from the island airport to the city mainland, I ask him if we're going straight to the apartment.

"No, I want you to get a proper introduction to the city first," he says. "Get a real perspective on it."

"But what about my bookbag?" I ask him. It's what I brought as my luggage.

"No problem, I'll carry it around. It's not too heavy."

"But it's purple with flowers on it."

Dad shrugs. "It's not like we're going to run into anyone we know." He laughs.

But he's right. Just thinking about it gives me a weird feeling. Then we step out of the airport and start to walk along the street downtown and instead what I feel is: wow. If you took all the tall buildings in Saint John and stacked them on top of each other, they would only make up about three tall buildings here. These are skyscrapers. Clouds could sit on the roofs of these buildings if they needed a rest from floating around all day.

Dad's idea of getting a real perspective on the

city is from the top of the CN Tower. I don't think I have a fear of heights. The widow's walk never bothers me, but this is taking the idea of heights to new heights, if you know what I mean. If the other buildings are skyscrapers, then the tower is an outer-spacescraper.

Dad buys us tickets for that super-high round part that makes the tower look like a doughnut on a stick and also for an even higher thing called the SkyPod. The view is about the same as what I saw from the plane. In one direction, Lake Ontario is there, pretty and blue and sparkly in the sun. But when I turn around, the city really does seem to go on forever. I can't help but think of a forest made of buildings instead of trees. The same feeling I had when Dad said we wouldn't run into anyone we knew comes back. A wave ripples through my stomach.

After we make it safely back to solid ground, Dad and I walk around more downtown. We walk and walk on street after street. There's so much to see everywhere. For supper we grab burgers but Dad tells me to leave lots of room for dessert. We go to a place called "I Scream" and he buys me their signature unicorn cone — a Unicone. It's a waffle cone dipped in white chocolate and sprinkles, filled with mini scoops of seven different flavours (and colours) of ice cream. On top is a marshmallow-sauce drizzle and more sprinkles. It's ridiculous — but in a good way.

"Better than a Lighthouse Cone?" Dad asks.

My mouth is already full of sweet deliciousness so I mumble, "Maybe," and smile.

"I'll take that as a yes," Dad says.

We walk around more and eventutally sit and rest on a bench for a few minutes. There are two squirrels chasing each other up and down the wide cement steps of a building behind us. They are black squirrels, which we don't have in New Brunswick. They look quite sleek and elegant (for squirrels, anyway) so it's funny to watch how wild and unpredictable they are, zipping and zooming.

Finally we go to the subway station and I take my first-ever ride on a subway on the same day as my first-ever ride on a plane. We switch trains, then travel a lot longer before we get off and come back up to street level. We walk to Dad's building.

His apartment is on the seventeenth floor. It came with the furniture — a couch, soft chair, kitchen table and two chairs, bed and dresser. That's all. It's like Karly was here and staged the place. He has his computer on the kitchen table as his workspace, since his new job hasn't found an empty office in their building for him yet. We video chat with Mom. I tell her about the flight and the city. Then Dad talks to her about the houses we're looking at tomorrow. Dad tells me that I can sleep in the bedroom and he'll take the couch. I'm sooooo tired from walking around all day, I crash early.

Chapter 16

Days since summer vacation started: 35
Days until Likely Departure Date: 26
Days until The Point of No Return: 38

At breakfast Dad says we'll be looking at five houses. Three are having open houses, so we can just walk in along with anyone else who wants to look. Then he has two appointments set to see places — one house that's for sale and one that's for rent. He wants me to be "open-minded" he says. Give the city a fair chance. So I tell him I'll try. And I will.

The first house is one storey, brick with a little porch. The front railing is a fancy scrolled metal painted a light yellow. There's no garage or driveway. I'd say the front lawn is about the same size as our living room at home. I'm sure you could trim it with scissors and it would still only take twenty minutes. The two neighbouring houses are about the width of a loaf of bread away from each outside wall. The only way to get to the backyard would be through the house.

We go inside. The front door enters into the living room and as it swings open it barely clears the end of a couch.

"Feel free to have a look around," the real estate agent says. She's pretty and is wearing plenty of makeup. But she has a plain navy dress on so she obviously doesn't shop at the same place as Karly. "Here's a bit more information about the listing." She passes Dad a sheet of paper. I notice the sale price. It's more than three times what our big house in St. David's is listed for! I try not to look shocked. I smile at the real estate agent.

The kitchen is behind the living room, then there is a little hall with three doors. Two lead to bedrooms. One leads to a bathroom. Dad and I peek in them all very quickly.

"There's no room for Jacob," I say.

"Well, Hope, now that he'll be going to university, he'll sleep on the couch when he's home. We won't be able to afford a three bedroom." This info is new to me.

Another couple that is viewing the house comes back to the living room, and with us and the real estate agent it's completely full. I suddenly feel warm and almost like it could be hard for me to breathe.

"Hummph. Hummph. Sorry, I'm going out," I tell Dad. "I'll be on the front step."

"That's okay," Dad says. "I'll come too."

"It was kind of small, wasn't it?" Dad says when we're on the sidewalk again. "We're not going to be able to get anything nearly as big as what we have now, but that was teeny-weeny."

"Teeny-weeny?" I repeat. I've never heard Dad say that before.

"Itsy-bitsy?" he says, and smiles. "Mini minuscule? All small?"

I laugh. I know what he's doing. I take a deep breath in through my nose and breathe it slowly out through my mouth. I told Dad I'd try.

And I really, really do try at the next two houses. Honest. But one of them has a lawn the size of a parking spot. The other is in a row of three houses attached together — and it's the middle one that's for sale. While I'm standing in the kitchen of that one, I start ticcing and the real estate agent swivels her head around so fast I'm surprised it doesn't fling off and into orbit. She stares at me, seeming to wait for something. "Excuse me," I say. She nods quickly, then turns around again. But the tics don't stop. I walk out to the small back deck and lean against the railing. Dad is still inside, upstairs.

"Hummph."

I feel a pinch on my arm. I jump and immediately look behind me. An older boy is standing there grinning.

"Hummph" slips out before I can say anything.

"Well, I guess it didn't work then," he says.

I have no idea what he's talking about. I think he can tell by the look on my face.

"Your hiccups," he says. "I tried to scare them out of you."

He's still grinning as if he's performed some public service. His good deed of the day. I don't say anything and walk right past him, through the house and out the front door. I sit on the front steps until Dad finds me.

Tic, tic, tic. I take a deep breath. It feels as if the tide is coming in down in my stomach again. And worse, it's swishing and swirling, like a riptide pulling me down. I know it, I can feel it, that not too long from now I'll be anchored here forever.

Finally Dad comes out.

"I know this isn't easy," he says. "But come on, two more to go."

I get up without saying anything and we start

down the sidewalk. Dad offers me a banana from what he brought for our lunch. I pass. I don't think I could eat anything right now.

"You know, Hope, way more people live in the city than in the country. Did you know the population of Toronto is more than three times the whole population of New Brunswick? I know this seems hard to accept because it's so different from where we are now, but this is how lots of people live. Who cares if our house is smaller if we're together?"

How do I tell him it's not just the house? I'm not spoiled. I don't need a big house. But I do need friends and people who know my tics aren't hiccups and I need space outdoors and I need the ocean.

I imagine kids who live here, who have always lived here, have special parts of it they wouldn't give up for anything, things I probably couldn't understand. They probably love Toronto the way I love St. David's. The city has power for them, an exciting, edgy energy. There is always something going on, there are always people around. I remember Willa telling me once about a guest at The Inn not being able to fall asleep because it was too quiet. They needed the city, the background buzz of things happening. At the time I thought it was so strange. But I'm starting to understand.

I think of all the TV shows where the characters live in the city. Unless it is a show that's set in the past, kids seem to almost always live in the city. And their lives are fun, exciting. They have friends, parties, special events, activities. They never have tics. They go to the mall and movie theatres and hang out at cute fancy coffee shops or juice bars. There's never an episode where they complain about living in the city. If they leave whatever booming metropolis they call home, it's always to go to summer camp, or on a school field trip to a farm, or to visit a weird reclusive older relative. There are hilarious problems that arise. The characters are always happy to return to the hustle and bustle. To me, none of it seems relatable — totally not my scene.

At the last two places we look at, nothing seems much different, except that no other people are there so the agents try to convince us even more how fabulous the houses are. I can't tell if Dad is being convinced. I'm not. I feel worse. I am ticcing like the second hand on a stopwatch. I almost feel breathless. And there are still waves crashing in my stomach.

Finally, finally we are done. We start the long walk back to a subway station. I haven't been saying anything. Just tic, tic, ticcing along. Dad seems unsure. He's looked over at me and smiled a few times, told me I was doing fine, put his arm around me as we walk.

"We'll figure something out," he says. "I thought it might be good to live right in the city, be able to use the subway to come and go, but we don't have to. We can live farther out, in the suburbs maybe, see what that's like. We'd have a little bit bigger place. I don't know about the commute, but we'll see. I don't mind driving I guess if it makes everyone happier. I can figure out a reasonable travel time. And maybe I could work from home a day or two a week like I used to. Your mom and I can talk about it."

Something inside me changes. The little waves turn into a giant tsunami-sized wave. My fear turns into something else.

"If you're going to commute, you should commute from St. David's!" I say — loud. Almost yelling. "You're the one who's doing this, you're the only one who has to be up here! You can move, but leave Mom and me home. Just come visit us at Thanksgiving and Christmas and stuff, like Jacob. Don't wreck everything. I don't want to be dragged up here! It feels like I'm being punished for something I didn't even do!"

"Hope," Dad says.

He tries to put his arm around me again, but I step to the side, out of his reach.

"I know that you and Mom didn't want to move either! But now you're acting like this is some brilliant plan you came up with — like it's something we actually want. But it's not! You can lie to yourself but don't lie to me!"

"It's not what we would have chosen, Hope, but now that it's happened it's important to see it as a great opportunity. And would you really want me to stay here by myself? Wouldn't you miss me?"

He pauses but I don't say anything. Of course I'd miss him.

"We'll get it figured out, Hope. We will. What's best for all of us as a family."

We walk quietly. I keep thinking, trying, almost saying something to apologize to Dad, but I don't. He lets me be.

On the subway I lean my head against the window. The car jiggles and shakes. My forehead bangs and bounces but I don't care. We go through station after station. Dark in the tunnels, then into light. Fast. Slow. Stop. Go. People off. People on. I can feel myself ticcing, but I don't know or care if anyone is noticing.

Dad is sitting beside me with one hand resting

on my shoulder. I read the big posters in the stations — for morning radio shows, an upcoming concert and a new energy drink. Then there's one for an insurance company that says "Life Isn't Fair." Wonderful. Tell me something I don't know.

I take a deep breath and I'm about to close my eyes for a bit, but then there's someone I do know. A picture of Anne and Phil is on a big sign advertising *Rise and Shine Canada*. I'd forgotten about Canada's Tiniest Treasures. I wonder where the show's last stop was. And what the prize is.

It really doesn't make me feel any better, but at least it's a little distraction. I can check the website when we get back to Dad's apartment. I don't live here in the city yet. I have to remember I have summer fun left in St. David's. That's what I have to hold on to. For my sanity, for dear life. And maybe, just maybe, there's a big going-away party we can help St. David's win.

I look at Dad and force a little smile. He squeezes my shoulder.

Chapter 17

Rise and Shine Canada has a fancy website with a big picture of Anne and Phil and a sun coming up behind Phil's shoulders. There's a wide bar with "Canada's Tiniest Treasures" on it along with a treasure chest icon and "Voting Now Open." I click through. The next page has tons of information that I try to scan as quickly as I can. First off, I can see that on Friday they visited a village in Yukon called Little Creek. I'll have to ask Willa how that went — if by any lucky chance a freak snowstorm whipped up mid-show. There's another button to click to something called "The Treasure Gallery," which I'll check in a bit. Then there are several paragraphs under the heading "How the Contest Works." I speed-read.

For the next two weeks, round one of the contest takes place. Two weeks! Round one? Wow, they're stretching it out. This is more complex than

I thought. And way less than ideal. Viewers can upload photos taken in any of the five Tiniest Treasures to show anything that makes it a special place. There is a limit of one photo per user per day. Each morning on the show a Photo of the Day chosen by Anne and Phil will be featured. It can be from any of the five Tiniest Treasure locations. So that's what The Treasure Gallery must be — all the pictures. Viewers can vote a maximum of ten times a day, every day. After two weeks, the two villages with the most votes will go on to round two. Details of round two will be revealed once round one is done. Of course.

I skip down to look for what the prize is. Great. Not a party or any type of event. It's some sort of custom-built park that will be designed for the village. There are about eight million details describing it that I don't read.

To summarize: Basically, there's a good chance I'll have to move before the voting is even finished. So I won't be anywhere near the place if St. David's wins. And the prize isn't a party, or anything I can enjoy even if it did happen to be awarded before I move. Whatever the fancy park is, it sure can't be built in a day or two. There isn't anything positive I can feel about any of it. Who cares if they win? If they do, it's one more thing I'm missing out on. Who cares if I even vote?

I flop back on the bed. I might start to cry. Okay, I do start to cry. I can't help it. I can't. I can't. "Hummph. Hummph. Hummph." I hear a siren go by outside. It was an ambulance, I think. I wish somehow someone could show up and help me. Respond to my emergency. Officially diagnose my problem — Displacement Syndrome, it could be called. Tell Mom and Dad the only cure is for me not to move. Recommend that I permanently stay in St. David's. Say the air is just better for me there. That's what I need to breathe. That ocean air. That's it. "Hummph. Hummph. Hummph."

I'd love to chat with Jacob. But he's way off grid making a new forest somewhere. I wonder if he knows he's not getting a bedroom in our new place. If he doesn't, then maybe he'd be a little less than thrilled with the moving idea too. Maybe he'd change his mind and come over to my side of things. Except I doubt it would matter now. It's too late.

I lie still. I'm going to skip brushing my teeth and putting on my pyjamas and hope that I can fall asleep. Then when I wake, it's off to the airport and home again. I can hear Dad chatting with Mom. Or some of it. Even with the bedroom door closed, the sound carries in the tiny apartment. I hear my name. I hear Mom say "Plan C" again. Then as the conversation goes on it gets harder to hear, and I realize Dad is whispering. I sit up to try to make out anything else he's saying. "I'm going to feel it out a bit, see what their expectations are, then do some calculations, see what I could offer," he says. "See what we can negotiate." Mom must be whispering too because there is a long pause when I can hear nothing at all. "Play up the benefits," Dad says. "For sure."

Then I hear my name again, but I've already heard more than enough. I don't know how Dad went from talking about maybe trying out the suburbs to talking about what must be offers and negotiations on houses. On one we saw today? And Mom is agreeing he should try to "play up the benefits" to me. Two against one. I know they want me to like it here. I know they want me to be happy. But. Yeah, but. But if everything was different I would be. As in, if everything was staying the same.

Maybe I can live with Willa at The Sea Captain's Inn. Maybe I can lock myself in a room there and never come out. It's the last thing I remember thinking before I fall asleep.

Chapter 18

Days since summer vacation started: 36
Days until Likely Departure Date: 25
Days until The Point of No Return: 37

My tics are so bad for the trip home that Dad has to sign some extra papers at the airport that have something to do with my "medical condition." I imagine if there is a section where he has to describe what is wrong with me, he puts something like "loud, annoying, but harmless, stable." If I was going to describe my problem I'd say something like "tics induced due to my life being wrecked by parents, not apt to subside." Or simply "Tic-tastrophe." I could really use some of the "Fragile" stickers right now.

I lean against the window of the plane and pull the top of my shirt up over my mouth. It doesn't muffle the tics much, but a little. The man in front of me turns around about fifty times within the first twenty minutes of the trip. I *accidentally* knee the back of his seat twice. The flight attendant sits in the seat left empty beside me every chance she gets. "You're doing great," she says each time. She gently places her hand on my shoulder. "Doing great." Even though it's the complete opposite. I feel like my tics are turning into Morse code for SOS. Except no one is deciphering the signal.

I finally decide to unwrap my present from Dad. It might make me feel better. He gave it to me this morning but said to save it to open later. Now counts as later. I have no idea what it is. The security person at the airport who watched it go through the X-ray didn't give me any clues either.

I slide the box out from under the seat in front of me. I open the card first. It says, "This is so you can finish what you started. Love, Dad." I have no idea what that means. I tear the paper off. It's a rock tumbler. It's for my sea glass. It's so I can smooth it by tumbling it in the machine. The glass would go in the canister that is turned by the motor, around and around. The bags of grit that are included would work like the sand — almost.

It's a nice idea on Dad's part. But it won't really work. It's not the same. The salt water of the ocean wets and changes the surface of the glass. It is absorbed again and again, ever so slightly. It reacts with the chemicals in the glass and gradually dissolves some of them away, leaving the tiniest little surface holes. The ocean's salt water is what makes sea glass so frosted and beautiful. And the rays of sun drying the glass on the shore again and again sometimes change the colour of the glass a bit too. Clear glass can tint to the prettiest amethyst. It's not something that can be replicated. It's like Mother Nature's secret ingredient. The rock tumbler would work on the glass to gradually smooth it, but it will never be the same as real sea glass. As good as Dad's intentions are, there would always be that one factor missing.

And maybe that's kind of like me and Toronto. Toronto is a rock tumbler and St. David's is the real deal. I need St. David's to be sure I grow up right. Hmmm, yeah, probably too dramatic and not true. People move all the time, I get that. But I do think a place can help make you. The environment around you affects who you are, I'm sure of it. And where you're "from" is important. It's usually the first thing people ask when they meet you. Your name and hometown is the information that people wonder about to open a conversation. Not name and favourite hobby. Not name and type of pet. Not name and best subject in school. I like being from St. David's, New Brunswick. There aren't that many of us.

"Hummph. Hummph."

If my old soul really is a recycled soul, then when I was here before on this earth I was near the ocean, in stretched-out space, not a city, I'm sure of it. I heard a fisherman say once that he was born with salt water in his veins. Back then it seemed like excuse-me-what? But I get it. And now I think: me too. I understand the idea that you are always connected to a place. It's the same as you have relatives who are people who are always connected to you because of common genes. A place can be part of your family tree too. Like the location where it is planted. Unless someone thinks about chopping it down. Or tries to transplant it when it's too big and its roots are too deep to handle the move and it wilts and dies. Yeah.

"Hummph." I am getting such a headache. I am overthinking. Way overthinking. But I am high in the sky with nothing to do but think.

"Doing great," the flight attendant says as she passes by.

"Hummph," I manage in response.

I know things that seem like a bad idea at first

can sometimes turn good. I mean, I've seen broken bottles left as trash on a beach turn into treasure. But I also know how long that takes.

"Hummph. Hummph."

I get the idea of taking a chance. I get the idea of trying new things. I can go on any ride at the fair, sample new foods, cut my hair, but this is too much new to try all at once. This is a surprise makeover that I wanted nothing to do with. This is all new things. This is a whole new life.

Chapter 19

We finally arrive in Saint John and the plane lands. Mom is pressed up against the glass door of the airport as I walk in. She smiles and waves, but she can't hide the fact that she's worried about me. I can see it. In fact, I can almost smell the anxiety coming off her when I go inside and she hugs me.

"Hope, I missed you. I'm so glad you're back."

"Hummph."

"So listen, let's go get a late breakfast — wherever you want," she says.

"I'm not that hungry," I say. I just want to go home and lie on my bed.

"Well, how about a quick stop at Timmie's at least, get a doughnut or something?"

"No thanks."

Mom looks at her watch. "Okay," she says.

It's a hot, sunny day. I ask Mom to leave the air conditioning off in the car and I roll down my window. The breeze is nice. She lets me sit quietly and watch the scenery go by.

It seems to take a long time to get to the part where the road is close enough to the ocean to see it shining like a giant blue diamond. Mom has been driving much slower than usual. But we'll be home soon. We pass by the road to the old lighthouse just outside St. David's. Then there's our village welcome sign. Across the bottom someone has added a banner that says, "As seen on *Rise and Shine Canada*. Vote Now!"

Mom seems to impossibly drive even slower as the road turns into the main street of St. David's and the houses get closer together. We inch along as if we're pulling a float in a parade. Then it all makes sense. The Karly-mobile is in our driveway. Karly's giant head on the car door seems to peek out from behind our lilac bush. She's having a house showing and isn't done yet. That's why Mom was trying to stretch out coming home.

"Sorry, Hope, she should be almost done," Mom says. "In the meantime, it's a little early, but we could get an ice cream from Frosty Point Light."

"Let's go to Em's," I say. We're already past it, but Mom can go back. "Then we'll know as soon as Karly leaves."

Mom seems unsure. "I don't want to seem like we're spying or anything," she says.

"Come on, Mom. Em's parking lot is around back. They're not going to see us."

She turns the car around.

When we go into Em's gallery, it's empty. It's weird, like she's been robbed or something. The walls don't have a single quilt up. There are no table runners for sale, no pillow covers, no mini quilts and even all the notecards are gone. Stitches is sitting on the only fabric item in the place, the little blanket in his basket.

Em comes in.

"What happened?" I ask.

She smiles. "Sold out! Can you believe it?"

"Everything? All since the show aired?" Mom asks.

"The website orders and calls started as soon as I got back from the filming and are still coming in. I thought there might be some response, but this has been beyond what I ever could have imagined. Hope, someone wanted to buy the quilt you're making for Willa when they peeked in the studio and saw it."

"Really?"

She nods. "I said you were good. And actually

you can use my long-arm to quilt it any time now. I'm busy piecing new quilt tops, so I won't be using it until I get them done."

Em turns to Mom. "I hope she keeps up with some form of art after you move," she says. "Quilting or painting or anything. She really does have a wonderful creativity. Hope's a natural."

I smile a little. Normally my insides jump around with joy when Em compliments my work, but it still seems like there's a big weight in my stomach keeping everything well squished down.

"Absolutely," Mom says. She puts her arm around me and kisses my head. "So, may I see this wonderful creation?"

Em leads us into the studio. Mom gasps when she sees my quilt. "Hope, it's gorgeous!"

Em starts talking to Mom about the details of the quilt, but I wander over to look out the front window. Karly's car hasn't moved from our driveway. The For Sale sign hangs from the post on our lawn, swaying in the slight breeze.

Stitches comes in and hops up on the window ledge. As I start to scratch him under the chin, I notice people leaving our house. There's a woman and two kids — a girl and a younger boy. Karly is right behind them, sparkling in the sun. They stop on the lawn and chat. The mom nods a lot at what Karly is saying. The boy sits down and starts pulling grass. Then I realize that I recognize the girl.

Oh no, no, noooooooooo.

It's Brooklyn.

Oh no, no, no to infinity.

Brooklyn cannot live in my house.

Chapter 20

Our house smells like cinnamon and lavender and candy canes due to an overkill of Karly's candles. Mom opens a window. I walk straight through the kitchen en route to my room for a nap.

"Hope, just a sec," Mom says. "I didn't know who was viewing the house. All Karly said was that it was a local family who wanted something bigger."

"It's fine," I lie. "I really want to take a nap." I figure if I'm asleep then nothing else bad can happen.

"Can we talk when you get up?"

"Okay." I keep walking to my room. It smells like pumpkin cookies. There's an indent in my comforter where someone obviously sat on the end of the bed. Brooklyn. I take it off and throw it on the floor. I open my window too. Then I lie on the bed. My bed. For now anyway.

I fall asleep.

I sleep for a long time and dream a million things. St. David's and Toronto all mixed up. I walk along city streets that turn into beaches then back into city streets again. The mini lighthouse of Frosty Point Light morphs into the CN Tower. So Willa and I go up to the SkyPod, then when we step out of the elevator, we are actually on the widow's walk of The Sea Captain's Inn. I climb up onto the railing. It's tricky to keep my balance. I teeter back and forth with all of St. David's below me. I jump. And fly! I am flying. It is wonderful. I am soaring over the ocean when I wake up.

The happiness of the dream lifts away in about a quarter of a second. It's like all the bad feelings I tried to forget while I was sleeping were hovering above my head the whole time, waiting to pounce on me as soon as I opened my eyes. It's like a dark rain cloud instantly bursts and soaks me with sadness.

My brain does a quick mini review of my current situation and adjusts my Mood-o-meter to "Gloom." I'm tempted to roll over and try to go to sleep again, but I'm really, really hungry. It's after supper.

I go down to the kitchen and Mom makes me some nachos with cheese and green peppers. She asks more about Toronto, but I don't want to talk much about it.

"I'm worried about you, Hope, you know that," Mom says. "Dad and I knew this would be hard, but you seem like you're getting overwhelmed. You're a strong, smart girl and I hate to see you not enjoying your time here before we leave. Please try to focus on the good. The city will be an adventure full of opportunities you'd never have here. Plus, you know we'll still be back here to visit every summer. And when you're an adult, you can decide to live wherever you want, the city, or here, or anywhere."

When I'm an adult. Yeah. That definitely helps the current situation. I can't help but roll my eyes.

Mom notices.

"Careful not to dislocate your eyeballs," she says, and smiles. It's her standard line.

"Hope, your dad and I love you so much. Please try to cheer up a little. Please don't waste your time feeling awful over something that has already been decided. Honestly, I know it's hard, I really do, and of course you're nervous about moving, but it hasn't happened yet. As impossible as it might seem, you have to go with the flow, let things progress naturally. Be happy today without stressing out about tomorrow. The one thing that you can change is your outlook — your attitude. Please. I understand you not being excited about leaving here, and even next summer probably seems a million years away, but you have to remember too that this place will always be a part of you. And you will always be a part of it. Your good memories of here can't be taken away. Just like people here will remember you. Your history here can't be erased."

"Very deep, Mom."

"It's true. And I know if you give it some time and really think about it, your sweet old soul can understand that."

I don't say anything. She comes over and wraps her arms around me. I lean against her.

I take a deep breath in and blow it out slowly through the teeniest opening of my lips so I don't cry. I can't help the way I feel. She doesn't get it. I don't want to feel like this. I don't want to go. I don't want to go with the flow and accept it. If there was anything I could do to change it I would. I don't want St. David's to turn into only a memory. Mom should know that more than anything I just want to stay in the present tense of things around here rather than being history.

Chapter 21

Mom finally says something that makes sense, which is that I should go see Willa. It's a good idea. If anything will improve my mood that will.

I walk slowly down the sidewalk. It's a sunny evening. A lot of cars go by. As I reach the driveway to The Inn, I hear Willa's laugh. It is loud and echoing and coming from up high. She must be on the widow's walk watching videos or something. I'm totally going to try to sneak inside and all the way up there without being noticed. I stay near the line of trees at the edge of the driveway as I start to walk along it. I'm in their tall shadows.

As I get closer, I can see her, or her feet anyway, up on the railing of the widow's walk. Two sets of feet are there. Lee's too probably. Because other than Lee, the only people who ever go on the widow's walk are Willa and me. It's our special hangout. Then I hear more laughter, but it isn't Willa. And,

I'm pretty sure, not Lee either. I walk closer. I can finally make out who is sitting with Willa. It's a girl named Claire. She's a highland dancer. Claire lives in St. David's too, but is a year younger than Willa and me.

"Hummph."

Willa and Claire laugh again — in perfect unison. I stop walking.

"Hummph, hummph, hummph." I almost can't breathe.

History — Mom was right. History. It's already happening.

There's been something I've been trying so, so hard not to think about, but here, now, even though everything else already feels awful, here it is. When I move, Willa will replace me. I will become who "used to be" her best friend. But I didn't think it was a transition I would see myself. I thought she'd hold off until I was gone. Oh, Willa.

Now it looks like she's getting a little practice in, or already holding auditions or something. She doesn't need this head start. She already knows everyone around here so she could at least wait until I'm out of here permanently to fill my position. I certainly can't look for my new friends yet. I can't put an ad on a Toronto new friend app: *Girl, 12,*

Friendly, Crafty, Ticcy, then hope for early replies. Or any replies.

"Hummph."

Oh, Willa. This isn't a preview I needed to see. Out with the old, in with the new. A seamless transition. I guess she doesn't want to invest any more time in a friendship that's almost over when there are fresh possibilities to explore.

They are still laughing and laughing up there.

Coming here was supposed to make me feel better, not a trillion times worse. I feel my heart petrifying and falling like a rock to the bottom of my stomach.

Claire stands up. What if she sees me?

I turn and run. I run before I realize what I'm doing. I can't possibly stand still another second. I have to get out of here. Before I cry. I know that's next. A sob is coming on that I know I can't stop.

I run back to my house, through the backyard and to our beach. I plop down on the sand. Then the tears come.

It's just one increasingly worse thing after another. I'm sad, but I'm angry too. I'm moving to a place where no one knows me and I'm leaving a place where probably no one will remember me. I'm getting replaced and erased. I feel like screaming and stomping my feet and throwing stuff around and slamming doors.

I stand up and go over to my sea glass. Why even bother? Who even cares? I roll away the giant rocks that keep the screens anchored in place. Then I start to rip the screens where they are sewn together. I pull hard and they come loose. I slide and lift them and shake out sand and bits of glass. I kick at mounds of sand with my feet, splashing it into the waves that are coming in with the tide. I jump and stomp on the wet sand. I pick up what bits of glass are exposed and throw them as far as I can into the water.

There.

By the time the tide has completely changed, no one will ever know that the glass had actually stayed here in this spot for years. Good. Just like me.

I sit on the sand. For a long time. Eventually our shore light turns on. I get up and click it off.

I sit back down and stare at the ocean.

Chapter 22

Days since summer vacation started: 37
Days until Likely Departure Date: 24
Days until The Point of No Return: 36

In the morning I wake because I can sense the bed shift with the weight of someone sitting on it. I roll over and open my eyes, and Willa lunges at me with a hug.

"Hope! I missed you! I'm so glad you're home!"

I hug her back and feel the excitement of seeing her perking me up. But then I remember last night, and my mind conjures the scene of Willa and Claire, up on the widow's walk, laughing and laughing. My mood reboots. I pull back.

I rub my eyes. Why is she here?

"Your mom let me in," she says, as if reading my mind.

"Willa?"

"Yes, it's me," she says. "You know, your best

friend for life! I sure hope you didn't already meet a new bestie in Toronto and forget all about me." She makes a pouty face.

I don't get it. Me meet a new bestie? It's like she's trying to flip the script, trying too hard. I study her face. She looks the same as usual — smiley, positive, happy, sparkly Willa.

"Hope?"

I wonder if she could have seen me last night. Or maybe Claire did and said something? Willa is just sitting there, with her lips pouting but eyes smiling, like nothing is any different, or that the only thing different is me and my delayed reaction to her, as if I've been the one to change things between us. She did have the lead in the school play last year and she's an amazing actress. Or maybe I'm completely misinterpreting things?

I sit up straighter in bed and shift back against the headboard. I accidentally hit Willa's thigh with my foot.

"Ow," she says, and rubs the spot.

"Sorry."

"Not your fault. I'm just sore from doing a major dance practice yesterday."

"You had class?" I ask.

"No, I practised at home, but I think I went a

little overboard," she says. No mention of practising with Claire.

"But hey," she says, "enough about me. How was Toronto?"

I shrug. "Okay, I guess. I'm actually still pretty tired," I say. "Maybe we can catch up later?"

"Oh." Willa looks disappointed. "Want me to come back after lunch?"

I think for a few seconds. "Maybe tomorrow?"

Now she looks confused. "Is everything okay, Hope?"

"Hummph." I nod.

I'll still hang out with Willa the rest of the summer if she wants to. Of course I will. But maybe this will make it easier in the long run, gradually distancing myself from her. It should make for an easier transition, so my leaving isn't so much like a Band-aid being pulled off. I mean, she's already started the process. Maybe Willa's onto something — no matter how horrible it feels to see her here now and know that I've already been bumped to second place.

"Yeah, just tired still. I'll come down to The Inn tomorrow morning."

"I suppose I can wait until then if I have to," she says. She leans in and hugs me again. "Come for breakfast," she says. "Mom's letting me make chocolate chip muffins. Okay? Promise?"

"Promise."

A few minutes after Willa leaves, I can sense Mom at my door. I don't roll over; I pretend I'm already back asleep. I'm sure she wonders why I sent Willa away; I kind of wonder why I sent Willa away. But it's for the best. I can't ignore or forget what I saw. I can't change how I feel. I stay very still until Mom leaves.

I try to go back to sleep, but I hear a little *ding* and I so hope it's Jacob replying to the message I sent the other day. He's maybe back at camp again and we can chat for a bit. No luck. The new message is Em's monthly newsletter, but below it I can see that Jacob did reply overnight.

"Hey there, city girl! Hope Toronto was awesome! Yes I know I might not be getting my own room, but hey, onwards and upwards. I don't mind a good crash on the couch. I have no idea what Plan C is. Mom and Dad never said anything to me about it. Maybe the C is for cat like they're getting you a cat to keep you company until you make friends. Or a canary? A chinchilla? A chameleon? A clown fish? (I could do this all day.) Maybe C is for camper? Like if they can't afford an actual house in Toronto you'll just live in a camper? Maybe C is for circus? Like if Dad's new job doesn't work out he'll be a circus clown (double C points there). Anyway, don't worry about it. Seriously it's probably some lame financial thing of theirs. Probably something boring. Forget it. By the time you read this I'll be back out in the woods. Bye for now. Your FBF."

Jacob is pretty funny. If I didn't feel so blah I'd probably have laughed. Who knows what Plan C could be. Whatever. I roll over in bed and eventually I drift off.

Chapter 23

Days since summer vacation started: 38
Days until Likely Departure Date: 23
Days until The Point of No Return: 35

So, the other wrinkle, besides knowing that she secretly has Operation Replacement Bestie well under way, is Willa's all-consuming determination to make sure St. David's wins the Canada's Tiniest Treasures contest. I don't even get to swallow my first bite of chocolate chip muffin before Willa rushes over to me in the sun porch of The Inn and starts talking about it at high speed.

First off, she doesn't care that the prize isn't a big party. Not at all. The real prize is exponentially better! If the village won the special park with the performance stage then she'd be able to highland dance there in the summer. They could have concerts with a pipe band and raise money to go to Scotland! Plus, she starts talking about all the great features the park will have — like a huge outdoor movie screen — and how it would be so perfect to hang out in. Not like a playground, but a super-unique place. It will have whatever we choose — designed just for us, she says.

I nod a lot and hope she doesn't notice any change in my facial expression when she says "we" and "us." Her competitive drive is one thing that hasn't changed. It shouldn't surprise me that re-gardless of what the prize is, she wants to win it.

Rise and Shine Canada is on the TV, muted as usual, but Willa is watching as she talks. When the little treasure chest logo pops up at the bottom of the screen, Willa takes the remote out of her pocket. She turns up the volume.

"Time for the Photo of the Day," she says. "Fingers crossed it's us."

But a gorgeous photo of the northern lights fills the screen. Willa hits "mute" again before we hear Anne or Phil say a word.

"Little Creek, Yukon," Willa says. "They had the picture yesterday too. We'll have to keep trying I guess. Have you added any pictures to the gallery yet?"

I have a piece of muffin in my mouth, so I shake my head no. I haven't looked at the website since

Toronto, let alone added photos. And I'm certainly not going to tell Willa, but I haven't even voted.

"You should add some. For sure."

I pretend to still be chewing so that I can just nod.

A couple at the table next to us leaves and Willa takes their plates out to the kitchen. She's gone for about ten minutes. She comes back in with a basket of apples that she adds to the breakfast display.

"Mom said I don't have to help anymore. Want to go up to the widow's walk?"

"Okay." Hopefully that means the conversation about the contest is over.

We are completely quiet when we first sit down. We often sit and take in the view, looking down over the village and out to the ocean. There's the slightest breeze. The sun is still rising but it's not directly in our eyes.

There's a boat way, way out in the water, a ship maybe heading for Saint John. Closer to shore are four kayaks. Les is out early leading a tour. Only a few people are on the public beach. Someone is in swimming. Gulls are circling at the shore, squawking.

"Best view in St. David's," I say, sounding like an old lady, or a tourist. But I want to break the silence.

Even though we often sit up here without chatting for long periods, today I worry that it seems awkward. "I'm going to miss this spot," I say.

At first Willa doesn't respond, other than to slowly nod, but then she says: "I'm going to miss you, Hope." She looks over at me. "So much." She doesn't say anything else and swallows hard like a lump was forming in her throat.

My breath catches in my chest. Did Willa feel she had to say that? Did I set her up for that response? Or did I misinterpret the other night? Go overboard with thinking it meant more than it did? Except they were up here, right here. Our spot. Our special, exclusive spot.

I don't know.

"Willa!" Lee is yelling loudly from below, out in front of The Inn.

Willa stands up and leans on the railing.

"Change of plans. Come get ready, please. Your dad decided to go in now for some errands and if you go with him I won't have to drive all the way to the city later."

"But the registration isn't until this afternoon," Willa says.

"He's going to take you out to lunch first. Please, come on now, it will save me a trip."

"Okay," Willa says, not sounding super happy about it.

"Mini dance camp," she says to me. "Workshops until the end of the week. Our teacher just found out and set it up because the instructor used to be the world champion and she's vacationing down here for the summer. I'm sorry I have to go so soon. I was only supposed to go after lunch, but you heard what Mom said."

I nod. But I have to ask. "Is Claire going too?"

"No," Willa says. "She left first thing yesterday to visit her grandmother for a few days. Sorry, but I better go down. I haven't got anything packed yet and Dad's never good at waiting around. You can chill here for a while though, if you want. Soak up the view."

She smiles, then goes through the little door to the stairs.

I do sit for a bit. The ship is still way out in the ocean, but the kayaks are gone — probably in the sea caves now. A man is walking his dog along the beach. The same gulls are circling and squawking. A woman is pushing a stroller down the sidewalk. A car is turning in the long driveway leading to The Inn.

"Hummph, hummph."

I sit, and I think. What I think is: So, Claire wasn't available to hang out when Willa came and woke me up yesterday.

Coincidence? Or evidence that I'm already a consolation prize?

Chapter 24

Days since summer vacation started: 39
Days until Likely Departure Date: 22
Days until The Point of No Return: 34

I act like a hermit the rest of the week. I leave the house just enough that Mom doesn't say anything about it. She knows Willa is away. But she doesn't know that there are other reasons why hanging out in my room seems the most stress-free option.

I thought about going to Em's, but Willa's quilt is at Em's ready to be quilted. I'm not sure what to do about it for now, so avoiding it altogether seems best.

Something else I'm avoiding is our beach, or more specifically, the spot where my sea glass used to be. Of course I remembered my dramatic destruction almost as soon as I woke up the next morning. And I felt a crackle of icy lightning shoot through my chest — a.k.a. a sharp pang of regret.

I know that the more I think about it, and no matter how long I think about it, the thing is, it's not something I can change. There's no rewind or reset button; what's done is done. It's not like I can go fishing for my sea glass with bait and a hook. I can't catch it in a net. But, for now, I don't need to see that empty stretch of beach first hand.

And the last thing I'm avoiding, which is the wildest of all, is pretty much all of St. David's.

I never would have imagined my last summer here would turn out this way, but so it goes. Because of the Canada's Tiniest Treasures contest, not only Willa, but everyone in St. David's, is in full-on St.-David's-is-awesome mode. Everyone is talking about it, saying how wonderful the pictures on the website are, reminiscing about great times here, asking everyone if they've voted. Businesses have signs up with positive messages like "We can do this!" Fran's Fish and Hips has a display of cool old photos of all of St. David's historic homes in their front window. There are new hanging flower baskets on all the power poles going down the main street. A free concert on the beach is planned for Saturday night.

Just as I'm getting ready to leave forever, it seems all anyone around here wants to do is remind me how fabulous it is. Not that I have any experience, but I imagine it's like breaking up with your boyfriend and then everyone around you not being able to be quiet about what a catch he is.

Mom made me go for a drive with her to donate two bags of clothes that we sorted through before the move. We had to hang out at Frosty Point Light when Karly showed the house to what she called "a very interested potential buyer." Otherwise, though, I've been here, in my room. It's crazy, but I feel trapped in here.

I knew I'd be sad about moving, but now I feel angry and jealous too. I don't like it. It's as if my brain and body are overcast with dark clouds, and thick fog and plumes of toxic smoke. My old soul is getting lost in it all, floating away, not able to navigate this. I'm anxious and my tics are getting worse. They're like this weird, steady drumbeat always in the background.

I can hardly believe I'm saying it, but I'd just as soon move right now to get it over with.

🐚 🐚 🐚

On Saturday night Mom makes me leave the house again. Willa is back, and she and Lee and Mom and I are going to the concert on the beach. Tyson

Crowley is performing. Mayor Rose apparently felt bad (not that it was her fault at all) that his performance on TV got wrecked, so although there aren't any cameras this time, he has a chance to entertain everyone. He doesn't have a stage. He's simply standing above the high tide line on the beach with another guy playing guitar.

People are sitting around casually on blankets or lawn chairs they brought. Lee and Mom sit on chairs, and Willa and I sit on a big beach towel right in front of them. Tyson had already started singing when we arrived, so we haven't been chatting really. It's fine. The thought has crossed my mind that perhaps Willa had to come since we were hanging out as a foursome. She is sitting right beside me on the towel, but I don't feel so close to her. It's an odd, iffy feeling.

Tyson does five songs, then he takes a break and Rose heads to the microphone.

"Just wonderful, Tyson. Thank you so much. And he's got more to come, folks. But first, seeing as there's so many of us gathered here tonight, I didn't want to miss an opportunity to encourage everyone once again to vote, vote, vote. A park like the one we could win would be absolutely wonderful to have, and we certainly couldn't ever afford to build the equivalent of what's being offered. As many of you likely already know, they announced on the show yesterday that we're at the halfway point of voting for round one. Only the top two villages will move on to round two. And, unfortunately, we're currently in fourth place. So, anything you can do to encourage more votes from friends or relatives, and of course making sure you vote each day yourself, is certainly appreciated. This is such a unique opportunity, and I'd like us to do all we can."

There's a "Yeah!" from the audience and then applause. Rose looks pleased. "I know we can do this, St. David's!" she says. There's more applause and some "Woooos," including a loud one coming from Willa.

"Perfect," Rose says. "Now, back to our fantastic music."

So, this fourth-place business is certainly news to me. If the village doesn't make it to round two, then everyone will calm down and I might actually feel like leaving the house my last couple of weeks here.

"Fourth place, really?" Mom says to Lee. "That's a shame. I hope they can turn it around."

Willa overhears her and perks up. "Don't worry," she says. "I have a plan that I think will help a lot. Starting tomorrow. And I was thinking that Hope could do it with me."

"Of course she will," Mom says, before I even turn and see Willa smiling at me.

Well, now I guess I have no choice, so of course I will. I smile back and hope it looks sincere.

Chapter 25

Days since summer vacation started: 43
Days until Likely Departure Date: 18
Days until The Point of No Return: 30

I meet Willa at the public beach parking lot after lunch on Sunday. It's a hot day and a lot of people are around. These are apparently perfect conditions to execute Willa's plan. She's printed flyers with information about the contest and how to vote. We both have a huge stack and are handing a sheet to every tourist we see. Willa says (and she's right) that lots of people have their phone out at the beach and can easily vote. We'll see.

After about an hour, I notice Brooklyn and Madison walking across the parking lot. Great. My already minimal enthusiasm for being here drops to a historic new low. I try not to make eye contact with them — we're quite a distance away. Tic, tic. They're probably just going swimming.

At first they don't seem to notice us, but before they reach the last line of cars, Brooklyn glances in our direction and stops. She watches Willa hand a flyer to a woman. Then she and Madison head toward us. Groan. "Hummph." Tickety, tic.

"So, Willard, what are you and Hickory Dickory doing?" Brooklyn asks.

I hand Brooklyn one of our flyers without saying anything, since she's right beside me. Willa hands one to Madison.

"I thought you were moving," Brooklyn says to me.

"I am."

"So, if you won't even be here, why do you care if we win?"

Exactly. Good question.

"Just because Hope's not going to be living here doesn't mean she's not still one of us," Willa defends me. She turns and smiles. I feel a squeeze of guilt in my chest. Willa never misses an opportunity to snap back at Brooklyn, but that didn't seem like acting.

A woman walks by and I hand her a flyer. "We'd love it if you could vote for us," I say.

Willa glances at Brooklyn with a look like see-told-you-so.

Then Mayor Rose happens to come along.

"So, what are you girls up to?" she asks, and looks at the four of us as if we are all here together.

Willa hands her a flyer. "Just trying to get more votes," she says.

Rose reads it over. "This is wonderful," she says. "You girls have such great community spirit. Keep doing what you're doing. I'm sure it's helping." She walks away.

A man goes by and Willa hands him a flyer. Then a woman and a little girl approach and Madison gives the woman the flyer she's holding. "Vote for St. David's," Madison says.

Brooklyn glances at her sideways but Madison just shrugs.

"I really want us to win too," Madison says. "It would be so cool. If we got the park, we could have outdoor movies in the summer. Brooklyn and I have been voting every day and we keep sending reminder messages to all our relatives telling them to vote. I can't believe we're only in fourth place!"

"I know!" Willa says. "We're trying to do everything we can think of too. I really hope these help."

"They should," Madison says. Brooklyn nods.

At the same time, a man goes by and Brooklyn hands him the flyer I gave her. "We'd love your vote," she says.

Then the four of us stand there without saying anything. No one is coming across the parking lot right now. Time passes. I notice a seagull fly over.

"That was—" Willa starts to break the awkward silence, but Brooklyn speaks at the same time.

"You know, your room is pretty cool," Brooklyn says to me.

Willa looks shocked. I think I must too. Then I remember I didn't tell Willa that Brooklyn had viewed our house. She must be wondering what the deal is. Willa might even think we were hanging out together, like new top-secret besties or something. Interesting. Kind of like her and Claire.

Maybe I'll let her wonder a minute or so before clarifying.

But then I look again at Willa's face.

And I can't say exactly how I know, other than I *know*, because I know Willa. I have known her since I was two, have spent more time with her than anyone besides my family. I can read her face in this moment and I *know*.

I was wrong. I am wrong. I misjudged, misinterpreted. I am sure of it now. I have not been betrayed. I am betraying myself by not properly valuing the time I have left with her.

Oh, Willa. I honestly think my heart skips a beat.

Maybe it is the feeling of it popping back up into place rather than staying sunken on the bottom of my stomach. It's like it springs as if it was launched by a rubber band.

"Girls," Mayor Rose calls. She is heading back in our direction with an ice cream from Frosty Point Light. "When you want a break, I prepaid for cones for the four of you. Large ones, whatever kind you want. Just a little thank you for your great community spirit."

I have also been betraying this place.

We all yell thanks to Rose. Then without missing a beat, I explain to Willa about Brooklyn viewing the house. I can read her relief.

"Are you going to buy it?" Willa asks Brooklyn.

"Mom would like to, but she says we can't unless we sell our house first, so probably not. Or unless her boyfriend proposes to her, but I really don't think that's going to happen."

Willa nods. Brooklyn answered her honestly like a perfectly normal conversation. She was actually nice about it. And I must say that it's also nice to know they won't be buying the house.

A woman with a little boy walks by. I hand her a flyer. "We'd love your vote if you have an extra minute."

"Just a sec," Madison says, and pulls Brooklyn a few steps away. They talk, then come back.

"We really want to win too," Madison says. "And these flyers are a great idea. We could help if you want. I mean, Rose already thinks we are — and we want to. Both of us do."

I look at Willa.

"We could take turns," Brooklyn says. "For the rest of the week, so you don't have to be here the whole time."

I can't believe it.

"That would be great," Willa says.

"If you give me a flyer, we'll go up to the library first thing tomorrow and get Miss Watson to copy more of them for us to hand out," Brooklyn says.

I pass one to her.

"Thanks, Hope," she says. Hope. Not Hickory Dickory. And I know I heard her right.

I look at Willa and smile.

This place has not lost its magic. I just stopped believing in it.

Chapter 26

Willa and I each get a Lighthouse Cone, then go to the beach and sit on the sand.

"Brooklyn was nice—" Willa starts.

But I have to talk now, to fix things right exactly this second. "Willa, wait, I need to— I'm so sorry. I've been doubting you, doubting our friendship, and I'm so sorry. I was wrong. I let feeling sad about leaving get the better of me and I was blaming everyone for how I felt instead of accepting that moving was beyond my control. I'm so sorry I haven't been myself. But since I came back from Toronto and saw you and Claire together on the widow's walk—"

"Wait a sec." She stops to think. "Last Sunday night? You saw us? Why didn't you come up?"

"I thought I would have been intruding, and you two were having so much fun laughing, and I thought I was the only one who went on the widow's walk with you, and I thought I was being replaced."

"Oh, Hope! No! Never. We'd been practising and we were so roasting hot, like, dying. And you know how great the breeze is up there. We went up to cool off. I could never replace you — never, ever. I know I'll have to find new people to hang out with after you move, but I'm sure not going to miss any time we can spend together doing that now."

I look down at the sand.

"Hope, I'm going to miss you so much I can hardly bear to think about it."

"Me too," I say.

I lean in to hug her.

We hug a long, long time.

I can honestly say that now I know what it feels like to be happy and sad at the same time.

We sit and talk more, then go back and give out flyers until our whole stack of two hundred is gone. Willa walks to The Inn. I head back to the beach and walk along the shoreline toward home. There's something else I have to take care of.

The post of our shore light comes into view first, then as I get closer my eyes automatically go to the place where the sea glass had been. It's such an old habit. I wonder how many times I've walked this way just to check on its progress. But I know it's gone now. The sand is smooth with only some rocks tumbled over it. And even if wrecking it all was an overreaction at the time, it's best now that it's done. I have to accept that. The sea glass really wasn't something that should have been in my control anyway. It always should have been something that I let go. Maybe keeping it in the screens was only a slightly lesser evil than using the rock tumbler.

Over the next few days, weeks, months, the sea glass will roll and spread. It will be pulled way out into the ocean and swept in again only when the tide decides. It may be gone years, but it will return eventually. Some pieces will be washed back to shore right here, but others will end up all along the beach. Lots of different people will find it — people from St. David's, and tourists visiting. And I know the pieces I started will excite them. So many of them are special, rarely seen colours. They will be treasures for them. Souvenirs. They are part of my history — even if no one else knows it. This is a new experiment, starting now. It's called going with the flow.

🐞 🐞 🐞

I forgot about Em being sold out, so it's weird all over again to see that her gallery's still almost empty. She has three new table runners and her display of notecards is refilled, but that's it. I go through to her studio. She's sitting at one of her sewing machines way back by the window; she didn't hear me come in. I'm about halfway across the room before she looks up. She seems surprised and folds up what she's working on.

Stitches notices me about the same time Em does and hops off her work table.

"Hope, great to see you! It's been a while; I was wondering. Are you here to quilt Willa's quilt? I've got it all loaded on the long-arm and waiting for you," Em says.

I nod. "But did you have any orders for me to address first? I know you're out of quilts, but I see you got more cards in."

"Thanks, but I'm all caught up. Come see if you like the thread I chose for you or if you want to switch it out."

We go to the big long-arm machine. Willa's quilt is in the frame, pulled completely across the width of it. Today the giant hand controls remind me of some complex exercise machine. I stretch my arms to prepare for my workout.

Em shows me the blue and turquoise variegated thread she chose, which is perfect. She also unrolls the quilt a bit from the frame to show me a wide piece of fabric she put at the top for me to practise on.

"So, have you thought about your design?" she asks.

"I was going to do random wavy lines. I think that will look nice and should be pretty easy."

"Good choice. I would make sure you keep them no more than the width of your hand apart. Some could be closer together, some farther apart. It should look great on your water section. When you get to the sand and sea glass part at the bottom, I wouldn't put too many."

Then Em gives me a reminder lesson on how to use the machine. It's a bit awkward to hold the big controls above my head, one hand on each side. I go back and forth several times on the practice fabric while Em watches. Wavy lines aren't hard to do.

"Now, just one more thing," Em says. "Years ago when women used to hand quilt quilts for babies or couples getting married, they used to pray for good lives for them as they stitched. Some quilters still do it today when they're making a quilt for someone who is sick. They think it's a way of transferring good feelings into the quilt. It's love they put in it that will then be wrapped around the person when they use the quilt. So, you don't have to pray, but maybe as you work, since this is a very special quilt for Willa, you might want to think of her, think of good times and think of good wishes for her for her future."

"I will," I say. For sure. I owe her for all the time I doubted her. "I didn't know people do that, but it's a great idea." A perfect idea.

"Quilting has many wonderful traditions and bits of folklore. The gift of a quilt is a timeless, wonderful, personal thing. So, now off you go. I won't bother you. Think of Willa and let me know if you have any problems. I'll make up your binding so we can get that on when you're done."

"Thanks, Em," I say. She walks out, and I take a deep breath and start to quilt.

It's not hard to have good memories of Willa. I remember sharing a swing with her on the playground when we were only four or five. The Halloween that we were both eight, she dressed up as Little Bo Peep and I had a costume made of about five hundred cotton balls to be one of her sheep. There were all the times we went swimming in the summer and sliding on the hill behind the school in the winter. We walked all the trails in St. David's on Earth Day and filled bags with trash. Every Canada Day we go into Saint John to see the fireworks.

We've camped in my backyard and hers. We've picked strawberries and raspberries and apples together. In grade five, on the last day of school before Christmas, we did a lip sync together, with dance moves and everything. Willa was graceful and I wasn't but she insisted we were both fabulous. Once, we watched a meteor shower from up on the widow's walk, which was so incredible I know I will never, ever forget it.

I keep quilting and I try to think of so many good future wishes for Willa. I see her going to school here in St. David's and then eventually to the high school in Saint John. For a second I imagine being by her side, going with her, but then I also think of her visiting me in Toronto. I think of us being together in the summertimes. It's hard to imagine what we'll look like when we're older, but I try. In my mind I see us walking along the beach the summer after we've started university and both being crazy excited to find a piece of what was once Willa's childhood piggy bank, smoothed and frosted and gorgeous, a perfectly polished piece of the sea glass I let go.

I can't believe how fast I get the quilting done. Em comes in and puts the binding on the outside of the quilt. Then we unload the quilt from the machine together and take it to her large cutting table in the studio. I notice that in the time I was quilting, she has either finished or put away the quilt she was working on before and started a new one.

Em helps me carefully trim the extra batting and backing off the quilt. Then she gets me the rest of the variegated thread to use to sew down the other side of the binding by hand. It's the last thing I have to do to finish the quilt.

"It is absolutely beautiful, Hope," Em says. "Be sure to take some pictures of it before you give it to Willa. It is a work of art and you might want a record of it for your portfolio someday."

"Thanks, Em. You're the best art teacher ever."

She smiles and runs her fingers over the stitch lines nearest the bottom of the quilt. "Don't forget to tell Willa about her wish too. She should think of it as she goes to sleep the first night."

"I'll remember," I say.

"When are you going to give it to her?"

"I'm not sure, but probably pretty soon after I get the binding done."

Before I go, Em helps me fold it up and finds me a needle to use for the hand-sewing part.

"I'm so proud of you, Hope. I'm really going to miss you," she says, and hugs me.

I concentrate on smelling Em's hair to keep from crying. I think it's coconut scented. I wonder what kind of shampoo she uses. Or maybe it's her conditioner that smells so nice. But I can't help it and tears do well up in my eyes.

"Thank you so much, Em. I'm going to miss you too," I say, and wipe my cheeks.

I can't let feeling sad take over again. One day at a time. Go with the flow.

Chapter 27

Days since summer vacation started: 44
Days until Likely Departure Date: 17
Days until The Point of No Return: 29

The rest of the week, Willa and I and then Brooklyn and Madison take turns giving out our flyers on the beach. We go in the mornings, and they show up to switch with us at lunch.

Other people around the village are putting in an extra effort too. There are signs about voting everywhere. Mayor Rose sent an email about the contest to the village mailing list that we could all forward to our friends and relatives.

I finally looked at the pictures on the *Rise and Shine Canada* website. There are gorgeous sunset shots of the ocean. There are endless photos of the beach and the sea caves. The Inn is there and so are lots of the fancy old houses we have in St. David's. Someone added some winter pictures too.

A couple are of the New Year's Day Polar Dip with everyone in bathing suits rushing into the ocean. (One has a little-bit-too-close view of a man with a beach-ball-sized hairy belly, but oh well.) There are also several photos of Sapphire, an ultra-rare blue lobster that was caught a few years ago and now lives at an aquarium in St. Andrew's.

Mayor Rose was interviewed about the contest on a Saint John radio station and for an article in the Saint John newspaper. It is the main topic of conversation everywhere in the village.

I think "Did you vote today?" has replaced "How are you?"

In the evenings I've been binding Willa's quilt. I'm very slow, but I want to do a really good job. I started helping Mom pack things in the house. We filled two boxes yesterday before Dad called. He's been calling a lot lately.

Mom talked to him a long time, and I did clearly hear "Plan C" in the conversation. Whatever it is, now it's a go. I'd actually considered admitting overhearing them and straight-out asking Mom about it. But I could tell she had rubbed her eyes a bit and dried some tears after talking to Dad. Then she said we could take a break from packing and wait until Dad comes home to help next week, and she went out to the back deck. She tries her best to hide it and stay positive, but I know Mom is a little sad about moving too.

On Friday morning I head to The Inn to watch *Rise and Shine Canada* and to see if St. David's made it to round two. (They better not just miss by a few votes or something, or I'll feel terrible for not voting at the beginning of the contest.)

Lee said Willa could leave the volume up on the TV in the breakfast room until the announcement is made. We don't know when in the show they'll do it, but there's a good chance it will be near the very end, keeping everyone in suspense and making them watch the whole show. I sip a glass of chocolate milk and sit quietly near the TV. Willa sits with me.

The show credits start and Anne and Phil talk about what will be coming up. The last thing Phil says is that they will be announcing the placings of the villages in the Canada's Tiniest Treasures contest in reverse order. The village in fifth place will be announced after the first news and weather update. Then the village in fourth place after the second update. Then the one in third place after the third, which by process of elimination will reveal the two finalists.

Willa rolls her eyes. "Pure torture," she says.

But all we can do is wait.

Guests begin to fill the breakfast room. They chat and go back and forth to the food, the toaster and the coffee maker.

Lee comes in and out of the room, wiping and clearing tables and replenishing the jam packets and cream for the coffee. When she comes in and sees the weather is on, she stops and stands beside Willa.

Anne and Phil appear on the screen again.

"Okay, so as you know, this summer we've been having a wonderful contest called Canada's Tiniest Treasures," Phil says.

He then launches into a longer-than-necessary review of everywhere they visited and how the voting worked. He then compliments all the villages on their wonderful efforts, says they are all great, and he hopes that just knowing how many people learned about each place will make them all feel they have won in some way.

This time I roll my eyes.

The camera shifts to Anne. She has an envelope in her hand. She opens it and pulls out a card.

"Without further ado," she says. "In fifth place is Dew Lake, Saskatchewan. It's a beautiful spot, folks. Phil and I enjoyed our stop there tremendously, so if you're in that area before the end of the summer be sure to check it out."

"So far, so good," Lee says, and goes back to helping the guests.

It seems to take forever for the next news and weather break to come on. There are so many commercials too. Finally, Willa calls Lee over. The list of predicted high temperatures for cities across the country disappears and Anne and Phil appear again.

"Guess what I have here?" Anne says, and waves an envelope.

Willa grabs my hand on one side and Lee's on the other.

"Hummph, hummph." I take a deep breath.

"In fourth place, we have . . ." Anne says, and opens the envelope, "Atkinson, Ontario."

Willa laughs. "Oh," she says. "But it will be so hard if we come in third. I think that would be worse than being last — if we just miss it."

"I know. But so far, so good," I say.

We keep watching the show because it's all we can do. The time passes slowly. Every commercial drags on and on. Most guests have finished breakfast now and there are only a few tables occupied. Finally, the weatherman says, "And that's what you can look forward to this weekend — lots of sun and hot temperatures right across the country. Don't forget to wear your sunscreen, Anne."

"Mom," Willa calls. Lee comes over.

"Hummph. Hummph."

Anne and Phil recap information about the contest again. They explain they will be announcing the third-place finisher first and that will mean the two remaining villages are moving on to the next round. Voting for that will start Monday. Details on what can be added to the website during the next round will also be posted Monday.

"So, who's curious?" Phil asks.

"Come on," Willa says.

Anne picks an envelope up off the table between them. She opens it.

"In third place is Four Hills, Alberta. Which means that our final two are Little Creek, Yukon, and St. David's, New Brunswick."

Willa and I jump up in perfect unison.

"We did it. We did it. We did it!" Willa says.

Huge relief.

"We did!" I say. We. Because I'll always be from St. David's.

Chapter 28

Days since summer vacation started: 50
Days until Likely Departure Date: 11
Days until The Point of No Return: 23

Willa and Lee come for supper on Sunday night. Mom barbecues chicken on the back deck. She has to use our big pancake spatula to lift and flip the meat on the grill, because the barbecue tongs are deep in a box in the garage. We also have corn on the cob and salad and garlic cheese bread. After, for dessert, Mom makes Willa and me chocolate sundaes with whipped cream on top. She and Lee open a bottle of wine.

They stay outside and talk. Willa and I go inside and up to my room. I'm going to give her the quilt. I got the binding all finished last night.

She sits on the bed. I take a large gift bag out of the closet and put it in front of her.

"For you," I say.

"Hope! You didn't have to. You're the one who's moving and I don't have anything for you yet."

"I wanted to," I say. "I made it."

She leans ahead and hugs me before reaching into the bag.

"A quilt? You made it?" She unfolds it so she can see the design. She drapes it across her lap and over the side of the bed. "You did all this? Not Em? It's incredible."

"Yeah, all by me. For you. One-of-a-kind design," I say.

She runs her fingers over the quilting lines. "The ocean and the sand and the sea glass. It's perfect. I almost think I should hang it on my wall instead of using it, it's so nice."

"Thanks. But you should use it. I want you to. And when you do, Em says the first time you sleep under it, you get to make a wish. You think of your wish right before you go to sleep and it's supposed to come true."

"Okay, I will for sure then. Tonight. And I already know what I'm going to wish for."

"That St. David's wins Canada's Tiniest Treasures? You don't have to tell me. I don't know if it cancels out this type of wish if you tell someone or not." I shrug. "I don't think it's an exact science."

"Don't worry, that's not what I'm wishing for anyway," Willa says. She leans ahead and hugs me again. "This is the best gift I've ever got — ever. I absolutely love it. I'll put it on my bed as soon as I get home."

It's exactly the reaction I hoped she'd have. "I'm so glad you like it," I say.

"Love it," she corrects me. "And the only thing that could top it is if my wish comes true."

"Well, no guarantees," I say, and smile.

I wonder what she wished for. I wish I had the magical ability to fulfill it for her. But I remember how I thought of Willa as I quilted, as I stitched in my best memories and kindest thoughts for her future. I thought only of friendship and goodness for her to wrap around herself. If you believe in magic and wishes coming true, then you'd think it would be those things that give them the power to.

Chapter 29

Days since summer vacation started: 51
Days until Likely Departure Date: 10
Days until The Point of No Return: 22

As soon as I wake on Monday morning, I check the *Rise and Shine Canada* website. It's been updated with all the info about the final round of voting. It's a shorter voting period this time — only until Friday morning before the show. The maximum allowed votes of ten per day per person is the same. The Treasure Gallery of photos is gone and instead there's a tab called "Tell the Tale." I click it. This time viewers can add either a written post (up to five hundred words) or a video (up to two minutes) saying something about why their village is fabulous or should win.

I think we have to do a video. Willa helped do the video announcements at school last year, and I know she helped her parents make a little advertising video for The Inn's website. Her dad edited it and it looks completely professional. We just need to brainstorm a good idea. I vote my ten times for St. David's then eat breakfast.

Willa and I are on the widow's walk. We're trying to think of what might be in a TV commercial if St. David's was advertised. In the New Brunswick tourist guide, the tiny section on St. David's shows a picture of the beach and sea caves. It suggests stopping here as part of a coastal drive. But that's something everyone already knows about. The shoreline was where the original show was filmed, plus there were probably a hundred pictures of it added in the last round. We're trying to think of something different and with a lot of variety. Or a funny format.

Willa suggests we maybe do it question-and-answer style with St. David's trivia. Or maybe we could give a walking tour of the whole town. Maybe we could count down the ten best things about St. David's. Film a flash mob on the beach? A music video? Interview a bunch of people and ask them all their favourite thing about living here?

We think and chat until we notice two people starting to walk across The Inn's giant lawn. We lose track of them when they are blocked by the large bed of shrubs and plants out front, but when they come out the other side, we can tell it's two girls. It's Brooklyn and Madison. I turn to Willa and raise my eyebrows. They keep walking, but when they get close to the porch, they don't go in. Instead, Brooklyn calls up to us.

"We came to hear what the new plan is," she says. "We want to help again. So we can win."

Willa and I look at each other.

"We'll be right down," Willa calls.

We sit in the breakfast room. It's almost lunch so we're the only ones here. Willa serves us each a glass of chocolate milk from the dispenser.

"The Inn is so nice," Madison says. "It's gigantic too — even bigger than it looks from the street. It must be like living in a castle."

"Thanks," Willa says.

Brooklyn nods, but then she looks down.

"I'm sorry," she blurts out.

It surprises us, so no one says anything right away.

"For not being very nice to you before, like Hope especially." Brooklyn pauses. "All that time — with the names. I honestly don't care at all that you have tics. It was just like once I started making a big deal of them I couldn't stop. It was mean of me. I'm really sorry."

177

"I'm really sorry too," Madison says.

I look at Willa. She nods.

"Thanks," I say.

"You might not believe me," Brooklyn says, "but I'm kind of going to miss seeing you around since you're moving."

"Yeah, me too," Madison says.

"That's it!" Willa says.

The three of us turn to look at her. None of us has any clue what she's talking about.

"What's it?" I ask.

"For the video!" Then Willa quickly explains to Brooklyn and Madison that we'd been brainstorming ideas when they showed up. "What Brooklyn said, about missing you. The idea of what we'd miss about St. David's if we weren't here is the perfect way to think up all the things to put in the video."

"Or what other people are missing out on," Madison says. "Like by not visiting."

"It could be like a video postcard," Brooklyn says. "Like we're telling everyone, 'Wish you were here. Look what you're missing.'"

"We could even start with saying 'Dear Canada,'" Willa says. "And then talk about everything we've been doing lately here in St. David's. And end with 'Can't wait to see you' or something. It would be a cool format if it sounded like an old-fashioned letter someone sent home from a vacation."

Brooklyn and Madison are nodding.

"What do you think, Hope?" Willa asks.

"I like what you're thinking, but what if it was like a fan letter? Like whoever is writing it is St. David's biggest fan?"

They aren't sure, I can tell.

"Or wait," I say. "Even better, what about a thank you letter? From someone thanking St. David's for everything good that's here, and for all the good memories?"

This is a better idea. Madison smiles and nods.

"Oh, Hope," Willa says. "It would be perfect. But wouldn't it make you sad to do since you're leaving?"

"No, it wouldn't be gloomy or like a wah-wah tear-jerker or anything. I mean, I'm thankful for all the good things here regardless, right? Just like you guys are." And really, I know I owe them all this. I want to do right by this place.

The three of them nod.

"And it would be a cool way for me to remember all my favourite things about here. I don't want to take over or anything, we can all do it together, but maybe I could be the one who is supposedly writing it — you know, we could even start with a close-up of a pen on a paper, and my hand printing out 'Dear St. David's.'"

"Dear St. David's," Brooklyn says. "That's what the video could be called. I think it's a great idea, Hope."

"Me too," Madison says.

"Let's do it," Willa says.

We talk through more details. The four of us brainstorm and make a list of all the places and people we should show in our video. We're all going to take turns reading parts of the "letter" as the narration. Then Brooklyn and Madison leave. They are printing new flyers to give out on the beach again.

Willa says she can film everything and then put the speaking parts in after. She can even film bits and pieces of things in any order and then we can put it together how we want. Her dad can help with the editing. My job is to think of what to say. Or, more officially, I'll be writing the script. It shouldn't be hard to come up with everything here I am thankful for. The timing is actually perfect.

Chapter 30

I'm sitting at Dad's desk in his office. So far all I've written is "Dear St. David's" even though I've been here almost twenty minutes. I figured this would be easier. I look at the *Rise and Shine Canada* website. Already there are eight Tell the Tale postings for Little Creek, Yukon. There's one for St. David's. It's a poem:

> Lobsters are red,
> Or sometimes they're blue,
> I love St. David's,
> And you will too.

It doesn't say who posted it. It would be cute — if it was by a four-year-old. Our video is going to have to be really good.

I take a walk to see if inspiration strikes. I head down to the beach behind the house and walk along the shore. I look for bits of my sea glass, but it must all be out farther on the ocean floor. I sit on the sand and let my mind wander.

A seagull flies over, then splash-lands in the water. He bobs on the waves. Up. Down. I remember that I saw some baby seagulls once, on the roof of a building near the high harbour bridge in Saint John. They were little grey puffballs, like a whole bunch of dust bunnies with beaks, wings and legs. One was outside its nest near the roof edge, wobbling. The tiny, funny, wildly cute thing — imagine a ball of dryer lint coming to life and trying to fly.

But I'm supposed to be thinking about St. David's. I try to get my mind to circle back to that. I stir the sand with my toes. I concentrate on listening to the ocean. I watch how the sun reflecting on the water looks like dots of light surfing up and down the waves. It is so beautiful. I'm so lucky to have the ocean here in my backyard. We're all so lucky to have it as part of our village. Of course! Which is exactly what I need to start with. I begin composing in my head. I know what to say now. It is simple and clear, short and sweet.

I zoom home. By the time I make it across our backyard and to the side door, I have so much to write down I'm scared I'm going to forget something.

The Karly-mobile is in the driveway. From this angle, with it parked so a row of plants is blocking my view of the wheels, it looks like Karly's giant head has grown right up from the ground. I wonder what — no, I can't wonder about anything or I will forget all the good thoughts for the video that I have to write down.

I swing opcn the door and run through the kitchen. I just miss crashing into Karly herself. I should have been able to sce the sunlight flashing off her rhinestone-trimmed fuchsia blouse like a warning light, but no. I brush against the file folder she's holding, and the papers slip and flip onto the floor.

"Hope!" Mom says, since of course she's there too.

"Sorry, really," I say.

And again I wonder what all the papers are about, but I can't forget, can't forget, can't forget the lines I am keeping in my head for the video script. Normally I would stop and help pick the papers up (and see what they're for in the process), but I keep going to Dad's office. I grab the pen and paper I left on the desk and start to scrawl.

I write and write, then read it over and switch a few things around to make it better. I think about how Mrs. McLean at school always said the first draft is never, ever the best draft. I read it again and change a few more things. I work on it for almost two hours until I know it's the best it can be.

Then my mind wanders back to Karly and what she was doing with those papers. Even though I tried not to stare, I did see one page that had spots for signatures. And I saw the word "agreement." When Mom listed the house, she signed an agreement to sell. So I figure someone buying it would probably have an agreement to buy.

But I'm not thinking any more about it. I know she'll tell me if the house is sold and we have a moving date for sure. I have to focus on being good and happy and thinking only about what's in my control.

"Hummph. Hummph. Hummph."

Deep breath. In. Out. And again.

Go with the flow.

After supper, Willa and I sit at the computer in the office of The Sea Captain's Inn. She has most of the bits for the video filmed. Her dad helped edit them so they are nice short clips that we can arrange in any order.

I know the four of us made a list of things to include, but what she has makes me think we had some weird ESP working for us or something. Or it could be because she obviously spent all afternoon filming every single location in the village and chatting with a significant percentage of our population.

I hand her what I've written. She doesn't say a word and seems to take a long time reading it. She finally looks back up at me.

"Oh, Hope, it's so beautiful!" she says. "I think it'll be great." Then she looks at the time on the computer. "Wow, we better get going. I bet Brooklyn and Madison are already there."

Chapter 31

We're finishing the filming on the public beach. It's sunny and hot so it's still pretty busy, but the four of us walk down the shore away from the crowd. The tide is going out. There's a wide section of wet sand. Willa, Brooklyn and Madison are carrying copies of the script and reading over their lines as we walk. I'm carrying the camera and a long, skinny piece of driftwood that I picked up.

We choose a spot and stop. We'll all be talking twice. I'll go first and last. Willa will film everyone, except herself of course. Brooklyn volunteered to video her. Everything should be pretty easy to film since we'll just be standing still on the beach, with the water in the background — except for the beginning.

For the opening of the video, I'm going to write "Dear St. David's" in the sand. That's what my driftwood is for.

"So, are we all ready?" Willa asks.

Brooklyn and Madison nod. I do too.

"Dear St. David's. Take one. Action!" Willa yells.

I laugh. I can't help myself. Then Brooklyn and Madison laugh too. I think we're all a little nervous, plus no one was expecting Willa to sound quite so professional.

"Sorry," I say.

Willa doesn't seem bothered in the slightest.

"Dear St. David's. Take two. Action!" she yells.

I start writing the letters in the sand. I really am nervous. Somehow I put the "i" before the "v" in St. David's.

We all move down the beach a little to a fresh patch of sand.

"Dear St. David's. Take three. Action!" Willa yells.

This time I manage to put all the letters in the correct order. Willa is standing behind me, filming over my shoulder to get a clear shot of the words. When I'm done writing, I turn around like we had decided so I can say "Dear St. David's" directly into the camera, and then continue on with my first line of the script. But I don't realize how close Willa is and when I turn I'm pretty sure she gets a shot of only my nostrils.

"Dear St. David's. Take four. Action!"

This time the lettering goes great. I then take a careful step away from Willa before turning around.

"Dear St. David's," I say. I pause for effect before saying my next line. "Thank you for letting Mother Nature be an honorary citizen here. Thank you for leaving her so much space to live among us."

"Perfect!" Willa says. "Got it." Then we tell Brooklyn and Madison what clips from our list we made that we'll be including — the beach, the caves, the trails, different spots around the village with big lawns and trees and flowers.

Next is Brooklyn. "Thank you for preserving and showing me your history so that I can remember our stories." For this we have lots of old buildings and houses like The Sea Captain's Inn and also the old lighthouse just outside of the village.

Then Madison: "Thank you for sharing your art, your food, your fun and your spirit." Here we'll use video of Em in her gallery, some from the craft gallery in the converted church, some of Fran's Fish and Hips, as well as some still photos of town celebrations like Canada Day and the Polar Dip.

Then Willa: "Thank you for your people, for my friends and neighbours." Here we'll show the dozens of people that Willa found and asked to smile and wave at the camera.

To finish, we are all going to repeat the same line. We're going in reverse order of before: Willa, Madison, Brooklyn, then me.

Brooklyn stays behind the camera to film Willa. I'm standing right beside Brooklyn. Willa says the line. "Thank you for letting me live here with you in this wonderful place." She smiles as she starts to talk but looks right at me when she gets to the second "you" and her smile disappears. She seems a little sad.

"Hummph. Hummph." Great. I realize that of course my tics were caught on video since I'm so close to the camera. "Hummph."

I turn to look at Brooklyn, and the old feeling of just waiting for her to laugh comes back. But she doesn't. Madison doesn't either. All Brooklyn says is, "How about we do that again, Willa. I think I jiggled the camera."

"Sorry," I say.

"It's nothing," she says. "This is going to be great." Then she yells, "Okay, quiet on the set! And we're rolling!"

I take several steps back from the camera in case I tic again. Which I do. The combination of

Willa looking sad, Brooklyn being nice to me and the four of us making this video together celebrating how great our village is suddenly feels very overwhelming.

"Hummph. Hummph."

When Willa is done, she takes the camera again. She records Madison, then Brooklyn.

All that's left is me. I take a deep breath in and blow it out slowly. I walk over to take my place.

"Hummph. Hummph."

Willa smiles. "No rush, just whenever you're ready, Hope."

I take in a deep breath again. "Hummph. Hummph." I only need to say one line. I only need to stop ticcing long enough to say one line. "Hummph. Hummph."

I look at Brooklyn and Madison then back at Willa. If this was a movie this would probably be the part where I'd miraculously get a hold of myself and overcome my tics once for all, then say my line with perfect conviction and clarity. But that's not what we're filming here. This video is a little bit more based in real life and there's no way my tics are stopping any time soon. "Hummph."

"I don't have to do it," I say. "Hummph. The three of you repeating it is enough."

"We want you to," Madison says. Brooklyn nods.

"Hope, don't worry, we've got tons of time. Let's just forget it for a while and do it after," Willa says.

"Let's go down to the caves," Brooklyn says. "The tide is perfect to see them."

We do. Since Willa has the camera we climb and pose every possible way. Willa takes some cool action shots of us jumping and cartwheeling. I take some of her doing highland dancing leaps. Then we have a rock-throwing contest for distance. And one for skipping rocks — whoever can get the most skips. (Willa wins both.) We try hopping back and forth across the little streams that have formed along the beach. We write messages in the sand. We draw pictures too.

Then I don't know who starts splashing who first, but once we start there is no turning back. We dare each other to wear seaweed wigs. There are brownish-green strands and clumps of it everywhere. Madison finds such a giant tangle of seaweed it dangles to her feet. She looks like a mermaid Rapunzel. I braid mine. Brooklyn also ties some seaweed around her waist as if it's a skirt. We laugh and laugh and pose and take turns with the camera.

Eventually we collapse on the beach. We are

soaked and sandy so we make beach angels. Willa takes more pictures (thankfully her camera is waterproof). A tourist comes over and asks us if we'd like a shot of the four of us together. The sun has started to set so it makes the perfect backdrop over the water. Then Brooklyn and Madison have to go home. Willa says she does too, so that she can get the video edited and ready to put up first thing in the morning.

She only remembers at the last possible second. "Hope, wait, I need to record your line," she says.

I look down at myself. I am soaked and covered in sand. My hair is a wreck. There may even still be seaweed in it. My shirt and shorts are dirty. But I've just had the absolute best night of summer. I look out at the ocean, down the beach, then directly at Willa.

"Thank you for letting me live here with you in this wonderful place," I say. It seems like the easiest thing in the world to do. It's like there is a pause in time, a split second when my feet seem to be one with the beach. I hear nothing around me. I only feel the air and sense the closeness of the water. I remember: If you believe in a place and you believe in magic then a place can be magical. Thank you, St. David's.

"Got it. Perfect," Willa says. "It's going to be so great!"

Then she rushes off.

I walk down the shore toward home.

I wish I could stay here. I know I can't, but I do wish.

I feel a tear run down my cheek.

Chapter 32

Days since summer vacation started: 52
Days until Likely Departure Date: 9
Days until The Point of No Return: 21

When I wake up, I hurry downstairs so that I can watch the video on Mom's big laptop screen. But she's video chatting with Dad.

I hear his voice say, "Still some paperwork so don't tell Hope quite yet. We can do it together on Friday."

He must have bought us a new house. But I'm not going to think about that right now, not until I absolutely have to.

"Hello!" I call before I walk into the kitchen. Mom has the computer on the table.

"Is that my seaweed princess?" Dad asks.

Seaweed princess? That's a new one. I have no idea what he's talking about. I walk around behind Mom so he can see me.

"Hope, I watched the video. It was great!" he says.

"It was," Mom says. "It looked like you were having so much fun!"

"I haven't even seen it all put together yet. I was coming down to watch it here on the bigger screen."

"You haven't? Just a sec," Mom says, and she pulls up the link.

Everything is very much what I expected. The writing in the sand looks good. The video clips are all what I've seen before. We sound clear when we talk. The only twist is at the end when we all repeat the "Thank you for letting me live here with you in this wonderful place." Willa put pictures of us hanging out on the beach last night between each of us speaking. Suddenly Dad calling me his "seaweed princess" makes sense, as there I am with my wild seaweed hair.

There are shots of us splashing and laughing, jumping and making beach angels. It does look like we're having so much fun — because we were. Then as the final picture, the four of us together with the sunset in the background comes up. I can't believe how big I'm smiling in the picture. We all are.

"It did turn out great," I say. "I didn't know Willa was going to use our pictures."

"Oh, they're wonderful," Mom says. "And look, a hundred and forty-three views already."

"And only four or five of those were me," Dad says, his voice floating in from seemingly nowhere. Mom clicks the computer and he pops back up on the screen.

"So, I'll see you both Friday," he says. He's coming for the weekend — to visit and to help Mom prepare and pack for our move. "My flight gets in mid-morning. I'll text you the time."

"We'll meet you at the airport," Mom says.

He says goodbye and I watch the video again. And again. And again. I've done my best to help St. David's win. I've made up for my lack of participation before. I'll vote my ten allowed times each day, but other than that the outcome is beyond my control.

I spend the rest of the week hanging out, having fun with Willa. When I walk home after supper on Thursday, I notice that the For Sale sign is missing from our lawn. It makes my stomach swirl and swish at the thought of what it means even though I knew this day was inevitable. My time here is almost done.

Deep breath. In, then out.

I'm going with the flow.

Chapter 33

Days since summer vacation started: 55
Days until Likely Departure Date: 6
Days until The Point of No Return: 18

On Friday morning Mom and I drive to The Inn. We take the car because as soon as *Rise and Shine Canada* is over (and we know that St. David's won!) we're going straight to the airport to get Dad.

Mom helps Lee with the breakfast duties so Willa and I can sit together and watch the show. We have the volume up when it starts, but after Anne says that the winner will only be announced at the end of the show (of course), we mute it.

The waiting is really hard, and both Willa and I decide to help Mom and Lee clear tables and replenish food to make the time go faster. The Inn's continental breakfast has never been so well-staffed. Willa and I wipe tables again and again until they shine. I'm almost thankful when a little kid trips walking back to his table and splatters a full glass of chocolate milk everywhere, since it means we get to mop the floor.

We finally go back to our table and turn up the volume when we see the last weather report on. Mom and Lee sit with us too. Then there are what seems like endless commercials until finally Anne and Phil appear. The Canada's Tiniest Treasures banner with the miniature treasure chest flashes across the bottom of the screen.

Willa grabs my hand. Neither of us say a word; we just listen intently.

"Well now," Phil says. "The moment we've all been waiting for is almost here. Anne and I had a wonderful week earlier this summer touring five fabulous villages located right across Canada. You at home voted for your favourites, and we narrowed it down to two — St. David's, New Brunswick, and Little Creek, Yukon." Then he explains, in long, drawn-out detail, all about the park that will be built as the prize and thanks the sponsors.

"But now, before we announce our winner," Anne finally says, "we'd like to take a little look back. Please watch and enjoy."

A video begins with clips and pictures from all five of the villages. Some clips are from the actual shows filmed there, some are photos that had been added to the The Treasure Gallery and some are bits of video from those uploaded to Tell the Tale. They play music and sometimes a line or two of dialogue in the background.

For each village we hear either Anne or Phil's voice saying "Welcome to" wherever it is. They show clips of each mayor. Kids and adults proclaim their love for their village. Then as the music starts to fade and I'm sure the video is almost over, I hear a very familiar voice. Mine.

"Thank you for letting me live here with you in this wonderful place," I say. The picture of me, Willa, Brooklyn and Madison flashes on the screen as the very end.

"Girls," Mom says. "Look!"

Willa squeezes my hand, but neither of us dare talk so that we can hear the TV.

"Yes indeed," Phil says. "So well said. Hear, hear! Thank you all so much for making this such a wonderful country to live in."

"Now," Anne says. "The winner is sealed in the envelope that Phil is holding. We will find out along with you at home, but we have been told the voting was very, very close."

"Hummph, hummph."

Phil rips off the end of the envelope. He reaches in, then hands the paper to Anne.

"You may do the honours," he says.

She nods and looks down. "The winner of our Canada's Tiniest Treasures vote is Little Creek, Yukon! Congratulations!"

What? Really? We didn't win.

"Yes, congratulations!" Phil says. "What a wonderful little place!"

We didn't win.

"Aww," Lee says. "That's too bad. I know you girls put a lot of effort into trying to win. And that park would have been great to have here. But they did say the voting was close. You should still be proud of yourselves."

Willa shrugs.

She hasn't said anything yet. I know she's really disappointed. I'm disappointed. I wanted her to have this.

"I thought for sure we had it," I say. "I'm so sorry, Willa."

"Yeah," Willa says. "I thought for sure too. And I know it's not the same, but I thought having this good thing to look forward to would make me a little less sad that you're leaving. Not that it cancels it out or anything, but still. Now it's just another thing that's wrecked. Of course not your fault. At all. But you know what I mean."

"Yeah," I say. It's all that comes to mind.

"It is unfortunate," Mom says. "And I'm sorry we have to rush away, but we really need to leave now to meet your dad at the airport."

"Call me when you're back, Hope, okay?" Willa says. Then she tells Lee she's going up to her room.

Usually Willa is pretty quick to turn a frown upside down, but not this time.

Chapter 34

Dad's flight got in early, so he's standing at the luggage carousel when Mom and I arrive. I figured he'd only have a little bag with him, but he's got all three giant suitcases that he took to Toronto piled beside him. Everyone else from his plane must have already left because there's no one else waiting.

"Hope!" he calls.

I keep walking toward him.

"Hey, you don't look very happy to see me," he says. "Remember me? Dad?"

"Sorry," I say. "I really am happy to see you. It's just that St. David's didn't win the *Rise and Shine Canada* contest is all. They announced it right before Mom and I left."

"Oh, I see," he says, and looks at Mom. She nods.

"Well, I have some other news that I think will make today special."

"Oh yeah?" I say. I look at Dad, then Mom.

They're waiting for me to say something else. So I guess I have to. "You got us a new house?"

"No, because we don't need one. We're staying in St. David's," Dad says.

What? I look at Mom. She nods. I look back at Dad. I open my mouth but no sound comes out.

"We're not moving," Dad says. "I still have the same job, but I'll be working here from home most of the time, same as before, and then going up to Toronto maybe once a month for a few days. You don't have to go to Toronto at all. Except of course for fun now and then you can come with me — if you want. But we're not living there."

This — I can't believe it. I'm not sure I understand or dare accept that it's true. And, wait, does it add up?

"Hummph, hummph."

"But I thought I heard you talking to Mom about negotiating for a house, and then something about paperwork," I say.

"Negotiating for my job. And the paperwork was my new contract. Once I knew they didn't have an office for me up there yet anyway, I started asking about working from here. A lot of what I do is on the computer the same as before. But of course I'd have to be in Toronto sometimes, for meetings, so I had to negotiate my salary. I told them I'd take a little less as long as they paid for my flights back and forth and for a hotel while I'm there. Your mom and I had accepted that if we had to move then we would — and at first it looked like the only option. We were ready to and it certainly would have been a family adventure. But if there was any possible way, we always wanted to stay here."

"Plan C was what your Dad and I called it — because it was a combination of him having the new job, but not moving," Mom says. "Plan A had been to get a different job here. Plan B was to move. Plan C was to keep his job and stay here. We just didn't dare tell you and let you get your hopes up in case it didn't work out. We really didn't know if it would."

Plan C.

"But our house sold. Where are we going to live?"

Mom shakes her head. "It's not sold. The sign came off because it wasn't for sale anymore. On Monday when Karly was there it came off the market. The guy who takes care of her signs was just slow picking it up."

"But you were crying when you were packing, Mom, like you were sad."

"Happy tears," Mom says. "That day on the

phone, your dad told me that us staying here was about ninety-nine percent. And oh, Hope, I wanted to tell you so, so badly. But I couldn't chance telling you if it wasn't a sure, sure thing. You'd probably never have forgiven me if I said we could stay and then we actually couldn't. Even this morning I wanted desperately to tell you, but I had agreed with your dad that we'd do it together."

"We're staying in St. David's, Hope. For sure. Done deal," Dad says.

It's true. I feel weak and then supercharged.

I laugh and cry and leap toward Dad for a hug all at once. The whole room seems to whirl. Dad has lifted me and we are spinning.

"I know this is where we belong," Dad says. He sets me down.

I start to sob, so loudly a few of the other people who have just come into the airport turn to look at us. I can hardly believe this is happening. Mom comes to hug me.

"Happy tears, right?" she says.

I nod. Then I take a deep breath and slowly blow it out through the teeniest opening in my lips.

"This is the best news ever," I say.

On the drive home (home!) I feel exactly opposite of how I felt on the way to the airport. I can see my reflection in the car window and I'm smiling the whole time.

I can't wait to tell Willa!

"You know, Mom," I say, "I can't believe you kept such a good secret. And you're probably lucky that Karly's guy was so long getting the sign. What if I had asked you who bought the house? What would you have said?"

Mom turns around and smiles and shrugs. I know the answer doesn't matter. All that matters now is this wonderful surprise.

I take in every bit of the scenery on the way home. It is familiar yet feels brand new at the same time. It really does seem wondrous and magical in the late-morning light.

As we get close to St. David's and the ocean comes into view, it seems to wave hello. I have never been so happy to see the "Welcome to St. David's" sign in my life.

Mom texts Lee from the car to tell her to send Willa to our place ASAP.

When we pull in the driveway, I can already see Willa running down the sidewalk at full speed. She's not even her typical graceful self, she's racing along so fast.

I'm sure Lee must have said that it was good

news, but I wonder if Willa could ever guess. She zooms right across the lawn and up the two steps to the porch.

Willa stops right in front of me.

"Tell me."

"We're not moving," I say.

"Not at all? Like, you're staying here?" She points down insistently.

"Right here." I point down too.

"Really?"

"Really."

She laughs and squeezes me tight.

"This is way better than winning the contest could ever have been!" Willa says.

Then we jump around and scream like wild. We're yelling so loudly with excitement that I'm pretty sure I hear an echo of us out over the water.

I notice Em look out her front window to see what all the racket is.

I wave and then grab Willa. We run across to Em's and burst in the gallery door. We startle Stitches and he scoots away, right through Em's legs and into the studio.

I don't wait for Em to say anything; I blurt the news out.

"We're staying! Dad can keep his new job and

work from home so we're not moving anymore!"

"Oh, Hope, that's wonderful," Em says. "I thought it must be something big, you two looked so excited out there. But, wow, you're not moving? That's such great news! I bet you can hardly believe it."

"It's like a dream come true," I say.

"The wish!" Willa says. "No, it's like a wish come true."

I turn to Willa. I'm not quite sure what she means.

"My wish. My quilt wish! It came true! I wanted you to stay. It worked like you said!"

"You used your wish for me?" I ask.

"I guess," Willa says. "But to me I was using it for myself. I would have missed you so much, Hope. So, actually it was for both of us."

Em smiles. "Interesting. Well, since you're here and we've got all this excitement going, just hang on for a second. I've got a little something to add."

Em heads into the studio and returns with a quilt folded inside out. The backing is a beautiful turquoise fabric with slightly lighter turquoise polka dots on it. She must have just taken it off the long-arm machine.

"This was going to be your going-away gift, but

I guess it will be your I'm-glad-you're-staying gift," Em says. "It's not quite done. I still have to do the binding, because I just finished the quilting last night. I was working on piecing it the day you quilted Willa's quilt. I was worried you'd see it."

"But, Em, you've been so busy and you have so many orders to fill. I can't believe you had time to make a quilt for me," I say.

"I wanted to. Have a look," she says.

Willa and I unfold it between us.

It's a little bit like the one Em gave to Anne on the show. The one I said was the best representation of St. David's. Except every quilt Em makes is unique, so the fabrics are different and the design is altered slightly.

The main fabric is the same colour turquoise as on the backing. The tiny squares are mostly grey and black and a rich royal blue, with a few bright orange, yellow and white ones mixed in. And, best of all, she quilted it with silver metallic thread in a freestyle pattern of loops and hearts and squiggles that look like floating clouds.

"I love it, Em. Thank you so much!"

"You're welcome. But now that I know you're not going anywhere I might be a while getting the binding on. I'll have to keep it here until I'm finished."

"No rush at all," I say. "You're right, I'm not going anywhere."

I'm not going anywhere.

I'm not going anywhere.

I'm not going anywhere!

Chapter 35

Days since summer vacation started: 56
Days until Likely Departure Date: 0.
Never. We're not leaving!!!

With the amazing news that we're not moving, we don't spend the weekend packing, but unpacking. All the things Karly had us put in the garage to help stage the house can come inside again, back where they should be.

We hang pictures on the walls. Dad's book-shelves go back in his office and we refill them. Mom puts a crocheted blanket on the back of each couch. I get the blender out of a box and put it on the kitchen counter.

I kind of forgot how much stuff we had. It makes the house a bit more cluttered, but also more cozy. It's like we're moving into our own house.

I spend the rest of summer vacation without a worry in the world. Every day stretches out long before me, then fills up with fun. My tics fade away. It's not like they instantly stop mid-hummph, but I gradually realize I haven't noticed myself ticcing.

I think back to when I last remember a tic, and at first it was yesterday, then two days ago, then a week ago. I'm not surprised they're gone, considering the stress of the possible move is over. They may be back again sometime and that's fine, but for now — yay!

With only three days of summer left, I get another surprise.

Willa and I are sitting up on the widow's walk. It's hot and we're just hanging out, really doing nothing. I'm leaning back in my chair with my eyes closed and the sun on my face. I hear a little sound like a guest has hit a wall in their room with something. A kid is probably throwing a toy around. Then only about ten seconds later, I hear a noise again, but this time it's more of a thump against the outside of The Inn.

"What was that?" Willa asks. "Is someone playing baseball?"

"I don't know."

As we sit up in our chairs to investigate, a little plastic bag full of sand flies up over the railing of the widow's walk and lands with a thud at my feet.

It has a small paper tied to it.

"What does—" Willa starts, but I've already picked the bag up. I unfold the note. It says, "Look down." So we do.

"Sorry, my aim was a little off and it took a couple of tries. My arm's still sore from planting all those trees," Jacob yells up to us, and waves. He's standing at the bottom of the front porch steps. "So anyway, surprise! I'm back for a few days."

"We'll be right there!" I call.

I rush down the million stairs, out the front door, and give Jacob a hug.

It's so great to see him again. He chats with both Willa and me for a bit, then she goes in. Jacob says we're going to Fran's Fish and Hips for lunch, his treat.

As we eat, I tell him about all the excitement he missed this summer.

Then before I can even ask him if he's disappointed we're not moving he says he's glad we're staying in St. David's.

"As near as I can tell it worked out better than ever. We keep the house here, but Dad has a free hotel room in Toronto whenever he needs to go up. And he said anytime he's there, I was welcome to come too. Even bring Adam and Dylan sometime and go see a hockey game. Best of both worlds. So, cheers to St. David's," he says.

"For sure," I say. "Cheers to St. David's."

☙ ☙ ☙

On Labour Day, we have a house re-warming party. It's a hundred times better than a going-away party could ever be. We invite pretty much half the village. Willa and Brooklyn and Madison and their families all come. And Dylan and Adam and their families. Em comes. She brings my finished quilt, which is every bit as beautiful as I remember.

Mayor Rose comes. She says she sent the mayor of Little Creek a box of lobsters as a congratulatory gift. He loved them. Then he and Rose started messaging back and forth, and now he and his family are coming to visit St. David's next summer.

Dad barbecues hamburgers and hot dogs, and everyone brings salads and casseroles and rolls and chips. We eat and talk and laugh and play Frisbee and hide-and-seek. For dessert we have a make-your-own sundae bar. Willa and I create giant ice cream, syrup and chocolate chip masterpieces and eat every last bit.

We get so full that we lie on the lawn until Jacob comes along and threatens to spray us with the hose if we don't get up. The party lasts all afternoon and well into the evening. It's dark by the time everyone leaves.

Then I walk down to our beach behind the house. It's still warm. The tide is in. Our shore light is on. I sit on the sand. I listen to the waves. I smooth my hand back and forth over the sand like I'm petting the beach. I stay for a long time. A long, long time.

When I finally get up to go back home, the tide has changed. It has started going out again. There is a wide section of wet sand that had been covered when I first came down here.

I notice a little something shining slightly under the glow from the shore light. It's small, the size of a pebble. When I walk closer, I can see it's a piece of sea glass. A pink piece — from my grandmother's candy dish.

I pick it up and turn it over in my hand. It's pretty and it's starting to round at the corners, but most of the edges are still rough. The glass hasn't turned into a smooth, polished gem quite yet. Mother Nature isn't finished. It needs more time in the ocean.

I walk to the very edge of the beach so the waves coming in are ending right at my feet. I throw the piece of glass as far as I can into the water.

Then I walk home.

When I finally go to bed I'm exhausted. But I can't wait until school starts tomorrow. I pull my new quilt from Em right up tight around me. I'm comfy and warm, wrapped in her fabric version of St. David's.

I close my eyes and make my wish.

Acknowledgements

Thank you to Shane, Eli and Tess for sharing my love of sea glass. I am so thankful for all the family fun we've had searching beaches near and far for pieces to add to our collection.

Thank you to my agent, Hilary McMahon, for finding a home for this book. Thank you to Anne Shone at Scholastic for her thoughtful and skilled editing.

To everyone in the New Brunswick literary and arts communities, sincere thanks for being encouraging and supportive of both my writing and quilting. And, of course, thank you to booksellers, librarians, teachers, students and readers for making all this possible.

About the Author

Riel Nason is a Canadian novelist, picture book author and textile artist (quilter). Her acclaimed debut novel, *The Town That Drowned*, won the Commonwealth Book Prize for Canada and Europe, and the Margaret and John Savage First Book Award. It was also a finalist for the Ontario Library Association Red Maple Award, and was shortlisted for several other awards, including the Canadian Library Association Young Adult Book Award.

When she is not writing, Riel can be found quilting. Her original quilts have been exhibited extensively. She is best known for her whimsical selvage quilts and bold use of colour. Riel grew up in Hawkshaw, New Brunswick, and now lives in Quispamsis, New Brunswick, with her husband, son, daughter and cats.